W9-BYP-475

DISCARD

SUSIE B. WON'T BACK DOWN

Also by Margaret Finnegan

We Could Be Heroes

SUSIE B. WON'T BACK DOWN

MARGARET FINNEGAN

ATHENEUM BOOKS FOR YOUNG READERS
New York   London   Toronto   Sydney   New Delhi

atheneum

ATHENEUM BOOKS FOR YOUNG READERS
An imprint of Simon & Schuster Children's Publishing Division
1230 Avenue of the Americas, New York, New York 10020

Text © 2021 by Margaret Finnegan
Jacket illustration © 2021 by Beverly Johnson
Jacket design by Karyn Lee © 2021 by Simon & Schuster, Inc.

For information about special discounts for bulk purchases, please contact Simon & Schuster Special Sales at 1-866-506-1949 or business@simonandschuster.com.
The Simon & Schuster Speakers Bureau can bring authors to your live event. For more information or to book an event, contact the Simon & Schuster Speakers Bureau at 1-866-248-3049 or visit our website at www.simonspeakers.com.
Interior design by Karyn Lee
The text for this book was set in Caecilia LT Std.
Manufactured in the United States of America
0821 FFG
First Edition
2 4 6 8 10 9 7 5 3 1
Library of Congress Cataloging-in-Publication Data
Names: Finnegan, Margaret Mary, 1965- author.
Title: Susie B. won't back down / Margaret Finnegan.
Other titles: Susie B. will not back down
Description: First edition. | New York : Atheneum Books for Young Readers, [2021] | Audience: Ages 8-12. | Audience: Grades 4-6. | Summary: Fifth-grader Susan "Susie B." Babuszkiewicz finds that running for Student Council is complicated, especially after learning that her hero, Susan B. Anthony, was not as heroic as she thought. Told through a series of letters from Susie to Susan. Identifiers: LCCN 2020052265 (print) | LCCN 2020052266 (ebook) | ISBN 9781534496361 (hardcover) | ISBN 9781534496378 (paperback) | ISBN 9781534496385 (ebook)
Subjects: CYAC: Middle schools—Fiction. | Schools—Fiction. | Politics, Practical—Fiction. | Anthony, Susan B. (Susan Brownell), 1820-1906—Fiction. | Letters—Fiction.
Classification: LCC PZ7.1.F53684 Sus 2021 (print) | LCC PZ7.1.F53684 (ebook) | DDC [Fic]—dc23
LC record available at https://lccn.loc.gov/2020052265
LC ebook record available at https://lccn.loc.gov/2020052266

To Mary

Dear Susan B. Anthony:

I have very bad news for you. You're dead. Really dead. Like, over one hundred years dead. Like, right now, you are dust and bones in the cemetery of your old hometown, Rochester, New York.

Sorry.

You are probably thinking, *What the heck? If I am dead, why are you writing to me?*

Congratulations! Even though you are dead, you are not forgotten! You are still remembered for being a brave and determined defender of women's rights, especially women's suffrage. That is the fancy name for women voting, even though I think suffrage should be the name for not being able to vote, because it sounds like the suffering you would have to go through if everybody thought your voice didn't matter one speck.

Since I am also a brave and determined defender of all the rights of all the people, I thought you would like to know that I am thinking about you.

Plus, Mr. Springer is making me.

Mr. Springer is my fifth-grade teacher. Every year he assigns this thing called the Hero Project. All of his students have to choose a personal hero. They can choose anyone they want, as long as the person is dead. Mr. Springer used to let kids choose living heroes, but then the live heroes kept doing horrible things and ruining everyone's projects. Luckily, dead heroes can't surprise you like that. We are going to do a bunch of research and assignments on our heroes and basically use them to learn stuff about language arts, history, and even math and science. Mr. Springer is always trying to find sneaky ways to get us interested in what he's teaching.

One of the main things we have to do for the Hero Project is write our heroes letters, and—duh—that is what I am doing.

Since this is our first letter, we are supposed to tell you a little bit about ourselves. So, hello! I am a Susan B. too. My B stands for Babuszkiewicz.

Don't freak out! It's easier to pronounce than it looks. Ba-boo-ska-wits. Hear how it rolls off the tongue? It's actually kind of pretty, don't you think? It sounds like something a bird might sing or that a Tupperware might burp.

Unfortunately, most people—especially teachers—

don't seem to agree on the beauty of my last name. They see a word like Babuszkiewicz on the first day of class, and their eyes get kind of squinty, and their voices get kind of stuck in their throats, and, after a pause, they say, "Susan?"

Sometimes it ends there. When I started my tap-dancing class, for example, my teacher did the old squint, throat-stuck, pause, "Susan?"

And I did the old "You can call me Susie."

And we both sort of pretended I was one of those Beyoncé-type celebrities who only have one name.

But that is not what happens here at Mary Routt Elementary School in the beautiful town of Claremont, California. That is because there is another Susan in fifth grade, Susan Gupta. She goes by Susie too, but she is original and hip and spells her name Soozee, which I wish I had thought of doing first, but those are the breaks.

This is the first year that Soozee and I haven't been in the same class. And so—until this year—teachers would always look at me, Susie Babuszkiewicz, with my regular, boring clothes and my goofy cowlick right in the front of my boring, not blond, not brown hair, and then they would look at Soozee Gupta, with her interesting French braids and her fun, hip outfits that often involve cool hats and sometimes even scarves, and they would give her the glorious name "Soozee" and me the name "Susie B."

As a person who cared about equality, I bet that this upsets you. I bet you're thinking, *Hold the phone! Why should she be plain Soozee and not you? Why should you be stuck with an initial tacked to the back of your boringly spelled first name? If anything, you should be plain Susie because B comes before G in the alphabet. It makes sense that the first person on the roll sheet should get dibs on being called by just their first name.*

I hear you, Susan B. Anthony, and there was a time when I used to feel the same way, which is maybe why I keep my distance from Soozee Gupta, even though she is a pretty nice person who I have no other complaints about. But then something happened, and I learned to really like being called Susie B.

You're going to like this story, Susan B. Anthony. It's good.

It all happened back in second grade, when I was in reading lab.

Now, seeing that you lived from 1820 to 1906 (which is an important fact that I am supposed to include in this letter), you are probably asking yourself, *Holy moly, what in the world is reading lab?*

Reading lab is this place kids go if they need extra help with reading, except that it is not really a lab. It is just a little bitty room next to the library with lots of posters of kittens hanging onto branches and file folders full of short readings that are supposed to help you read better. I was in reading lab until the end of third grade.

This is nothing to be ashamed of, by the way, and if people tell you otherwise, you are allowed to give them a good stink eye and tell them to park their prejudice at the door. Some brains just need more help with reading than others. I needed help because my brain is easily distracted by—wait—is that a butterfly?

Ha! There wasn't really a butterfly. I was just trying to give you a sense of how easily my brain can get off course when it is not interested in something. But I'm interested in this, so don't worry. Writing and reading are things I can do forever and ever because I love them so much. It was the learning them that I didn't like because—what the heck?—English does not make any sense at all! What kind of language, for example, has one way to pronounce three entirely different words, like "pair," "pare," and "pear"? Honestly, I'm still not sure which one is which. Would you like to eat a pare? Don't ask me! Or, in what kind of world would "through" be pronounced throo and "cough" be pronounced coff? It makes no sense! Look hard at those words! They are exactly the same except for the beginning letters. They should at least rhyme! And don't get me started on "dough"!

Luckily for me, once my *Is that a butterfly?* brain was finally able to get past all that boring stuff, I was able to catch up. Now I can read as good as anyone. But I'm still a terrible speller. (Confession: only last year did I finally remember how to spell my own last name. Then again, I think it might take anyone a long time to remember how to spell Babuszkiewicz because there are a crazy lot of consonants in there.)

It is because I am such a terrible speller that I get to write my letters to you on a tablet and use spell-check. Other kids can write their letters on tablets too. Everyone in our class gets one. But for me, writing on a tablet is an actual *right*. It's what you call an accommodation, on account of my butterfly brain. Accommodations help make things fair for everybody.

Which brings me back to reading lab and how I learned to love being called Susie B. Don't drift off, Susan B. Anthony. I promise you'll like this.

Anyway, it was one of my very first days of reading lab. I was there with Carson, who still goes to reading lab because he is a work in progress like the rest of us. The reading specialist pointed us toward this one particular file cabinet and told us to pick a reading that looked interesting.

I was flipping through all these different readings when I saw one called "Susan B. Fights On." I still remember the name because I was thinking: Gosh, is this about me? Did the reading specialist hide this here for me to find? Is it a present? Did she make one for all of us, each with our own name on it? Is it supposed to make us feel better about going to reading lab even though we shouldn't feel bad in the first place? And—most importantly—what the heck am I fighting on about this time?

I told all that to Carson, and his eyes were like, *Ba-boing! I want one too!* But his brain is even more butterflyish than mine, so he started flipping through all the files and trying to find a reading with his name on it. He climbed right onto a chair so he could pull files down from the high cupboard.

When the reading specialist found us, she said, "For heaven's sake"—that was a real favorite phrase of hers.

She asked us what we were doing, and I explained right away. Then she admitted that she had not been cool enough to make us each our own special readings, but that I still might like "Susan B. Fights On" since it was about a very interesting woman named—wait for it—Susan B. Anthony! Ha, ha! That's you!

Now, don't get mad, but at first I was a little bummed. I liked believing that the reading specialist had done all this work to figure out who I was and how I like to fight on about things. It made me feel special. Since I have always suspected that I am actually a little fabulous, that was pretty cool. But my disappointment passed quickly because I realized that the reading specialist was right. You were very interesting, Susan B. Anthony!

When most of the women of your time were focused on getting married and having kids, you were all, "How in the world can we say we fought a revolution over taxation without representation and then deny women the right to vote? How can we harp on about freedom and liberty and then say to women, 'No freedom or liberty for you'? I will not accept this! I will spend my life fighting for women's rights, and I will not give up until every woman in this land has the same chance to vote as your common, garden-variety man."

When I finished the reading, I was blown away. I learned something important. I learned that being a Susie B. wasn't something to be annoyed by. It was something to be proud of. Being a Susie B. meant being a Susan B. Anthony, a fighter of good fights. And who wouldn't want to be that?

So this year, when Mr. Springer read roll for the first time and did the old *Susan Buuuuuuu . . . Susan*, I told him, "Hey, Mr. Springer, just call me Susie B. Everybody else does. It's fine with me."

And he was all, "Okay, Susie B.!"

See? I told you that you would like that story.

Dear Susan B. Anthony:

We went to the media lab today to do research about our heroes, and now that I have told you about me, I am supposed to tell you about you. But I am not supposed to go on for pages and pages, because that is not what the Hero Project is all about, and Mr. Springer has a full life, after all. (At least that's what he said.) He cannot be expected to read superlong hero letters from students, even if the students really like to read and write. We should just get to the point and stick to the point because it is important to be able to follow directions.

So here is a tiny bit amount of information about you.

You were born in Adams, Massachusetts, you had lots of siblings, and you were raised a Quaker. Quakers believe that every single person has an Inner Light in them, which is really a tiny spark of God's spirit. That Inner Light makes all people holy, and it means that nobody is better than anybody else. So they don't have ministers because they believe God inspires everyone equally, and they don't think boys are better than girls, or that one race of people is better than another race of people, or that anybody should be killing anybody in wars because when you kill people, you kill their divine sparks, and that means you are basically killing God.

I was telling my mom and my brother, Lock, all this when I came home from school. We were at the table eating a very boring snack of raw vegetables and hummus because my mother says too much refined starch makes my butterfly brain really flappy.

Although I will never admit this to her, it is possible she is right. Once, I ate a giant chocolate Santa Claus on Christmas morning, and I couldn't sit still for four hours. My grandparents were worried that I was seriously disturbed, but my parents reminded them that Lock was exactly the same way when he was my age.

And I was like, "Give me a break, Grandsters! It's Christmas!"

And my parents and grandparents were like, "Don't get snotty with us, little miss!"

And I was like, "ME WANT MORE SUGAR!"

Anyway, Lock said that he already knew all about Quakers. Of course, we had to believe him. The whole reason we call him Lock and not his real name, Tyler, is because his mind protects information like locks protect bicycles. But—like me—he has to be interested in the information for the lock effect to work. Otherwise, he is like an open lock, and you know nothing is going to stay safe with that. That is the reason why he is having a little bit of a problem at community college. He does really well in the classes he finds interesting, but he doesn't do so well in the classes he finds boring. Since he is trying to transfer to a university, he's worried that his flip-floppy grades will make all the schools he applies to reject him.

The point is, Lock thinks it's good that I am learning about Quakers because they are very cool. They opposed slavery. They supported the civil rights movement. Apparently, if you are ever in doubt about whether something might be evil, you should find out what the Quakers think.

"Time always proves them right," Lock told me. He really said that! That is a true quote. I wrote it down in my little notebook that I always pull out when people say something I want to remember later.

Mom opened her mouth to talk, but since I had not quite finished all that I had to say, I quickly added my two cents. "You might be right, Lock, but did you also know that Quakers are big shunners? Susan B.

Anthony's dad was a Quaker, but her mom was not, and so the Quakers were just all, 'You married outside the Quakers, and so now we are shunning you. Goodbye and amen!'" (These are not direct quotes, by the way. The Quakers did not actually say that, and neither did I. But that was the gist of things in both cases, and you are just going to have to trust me on that.)

Lock was very surprised and impressed that I knew something that he didn't know. I could tell because he didn't answer me, and Lock always has an answer.

Mom agreed that I was being very interesting. And I could tell that she meant it because she wasn't looking at her phone. I personally do not have a phone . . . or a gaming system. I barely even get to watch TV. The only technology I am allowed is my school tablet, and that has lots of restrictions on it. My parents say too much electronics will make it harder for my butterfly brain to focus on what is important, and Lock says they are right because they learned the hard way with him. But I say that being a fifth grader without her own tech is being a fifth grader who is living in the Dark Ages. So, naturally, this is one of the many injustices that I must constantly battle.

But I did not want to bring up that sore subject at

that time. I wanted to focus on the fact that I can be as much of a lock as Lock. And having locked them with my good story about the Quakers shunning people, I went in for the double lockdown of topping that fascinating piece of information with another. I explained that even though the Quakers shunned your dad, Susan B. Anthony, they still let you and your brothers and sisters join their community, so at least the Quakers didn't pass down shunnings.

Lock kind of nodded, like, *Good job, little sis. You're a chip off the old Lock.* Then he asked if they are still big shunners.

That was something that I didn't know, so we just let the conversation drop.

Here is my question for you, Susan B. Anthony: What did you think about this shunning business? Did you accept it? Or did you think that it was mean? It sounds mean, and I think that if everyone has an Inner Light, then you shouldn't shun anyone. Instead, you should be nice to everyone, even mean people. Although, to be honest, I am not always nice to mean people, but that is only because I have never thought about this Inner Light stuff. It seems to me that, when it comes to mean people, you've sometimes got to fight mean with mean.

For example, there is a mean kid in my class named Chloe Howard. My secret name for her is "Old Fakey Fake." She pretends to be nice when teachers are around, but as soon as teachers leave, she'll say something mean, or she'll say something that doesn't sound mean but that infects you with a mysterious sense of worry.

One time, before I knew she was such a fakey fake, she said something like, "You're so lucky that you are bad at spelling. It is so much better to get to write stuff on the computer all the time." Then she looked over at the three Rs, otherwise known as Rachelle, Rachel, and Rose. They are her little band of toadies. They follow her everywhere. When she said I was lucky to spell badly, they all got these sneaky little smiles on their faces.

See what I mean? Technically, Chloe had not said anything mean, especially since I am always saying that I can spell as well as a can of alphabet soup. But the way she said it, and the way she looked at her friends . . . It made me feel like a bicycle tire with a slow leak. As the day went on, I kept feeling flatter, and flatter, and flatter until all I wanted to do was crawl under my covers and cry about how terrible I am at spelling.

Not even Joselyn Salazar could make me feel better.

Joselyn is my best spark. I am guessing that you do not know what a best spark is, and that is all right, Susan B. Anthony. Don't feel bad! You were dead way before I even invented that term, which was just today. A best spark is like a best friend, but better. A best spark *sparks* you so that you can keep on going even when things get rough.

You get it, right? I know you do because you had a best spark too. Her name was Elizabeth Cady Stanton. She would always help you with your writing because you did not have quite the flair for it that Elizabeth did, and you would always help her by babysitting her seven children so that she could write stuff and not just drown in dirty diapers.

Joselyn and I have been best sparks since second grade, when she would help me at reading time and I would fill her in on the plot of this show about a superhero who can remember every book ever written, even the ones she hasn't read—even in languages she doesn't know. I only got to watch it because Lock and I would secretly stream it on his computer, but Joselyn had never seen it since her mom believes screens rot people's brains. So it was a good exchange that brought us together, and the screen part keeps us together even now. When you are the only two kids at school who don't have Disney+, you have a lot to bond over.

Just yesterday Joselyn and I were laughing our heads off about her cat, Fred, who pees in the toilet just like a person. Really! I've seen him! He figured it out all by himself! While we were laughing, we started practicing this new combination that we recently learned in our tap-dancing class. We didn't have our tap shoes, but we never let that stop us. We were doing shuffles followed by single buffaloes, and I was doing some very creative arm movements to spice it up. Joselyn was not doing the arm movements, but her cool worry-doll earrings that her grandma brought her from Guatemala were flapping like crazy, which was almost the same thing.

Of course, Old Fakey Fake had to ruin it. She and the three Rs walked by us. A second later, Chloe said something like, "Won't it be great when we go to middle school next year and are surrounded by more *mature* people?" And she said it super loudly to make sure we would hear her.

For a second, Joselyn and I froze and looked at each other, embarrassed. I remembered how Lock always tells me that I should treat Fakey Fake like she is a gnat too insignificant to bother swatting, but I'm used to fighting mean with mean and also snarky with snarky. So I swatted.

I yelled, "Oh, that's not maturity you're thinking of. It's body odor."

Old Fakey Fake kept walking, but her shoulders and butt got all stiff, making her legs straight as toothpicks.

I fell onto the ground in hysterics. Joselyn sat next to me. She laughed a little, but she kept her eye on Chloe and her friends. When they were gone, she slumped down and relaxed.

I put my sweaty hand on her arm and told her it really was true. Lock told me. Everyone stinks in middle school.

"No," she said very seriously. I thought maybe I was being too silly for Joselyn (it happens!), so I took some deep breaths and collected myself.

Joselyn gave me a stern look and reminded me that Lock has not been in middle school for a long time, but her sister, Melissa, is in middle school now. She said Melissa has never said that everyone stinks. Then she got a very smiley look in her eyes and said, "But Melissa probably just can't smell anybody else over her own B.O."

And that set us off laughing even more!

But don't worry, Susan B. Anthony. It was all in good fun. As a sister yourself, you probably know that siblings are allowed to joke about each other. Joselyn says it is one of the few benefits of even having siblings, but then she is not tight with Melissa like I am with Lock.

I will tell you this, though, Susan B. Anthony. Old Fakey Fake is sneakier than her perfect posture makes her look. Her words are time bombs that silently tick, tick, tick in your head until—boom—they are all you can think about. After my laugh attack with Joselyn, I hadn't given Fakey Fake another thought, but when I got into bed, I suddenly remembered what she said. *Won't it be great when we go to middle school next year and are surrounded by more mature people?* And then I couldn't think about anything else. I wondered: What if I'm not mature enough for middle school? What if people will think tap dancing is babyish? What if they think Joselyn and I are babyish? *Am I babyish?*

Sometimes I think that maybe I am. Just recently I noticed that lots of fifth graders don't really play at recess anymore. They'll do sports, or they'll walk around and talk about boring stuff, but they won't *play*. And if you mention that you still like to take out your stuffed animals sometimes, or that you thought it might be fun to play Percy Jackson—like you did for a good chunk of last year without anyone caring one way or another—they will look at you like you said something wrong, something that might get you in trouble, that might get them in trouble if they were to agree.

This has even started to happen with Joselyn some-times. We'll be having a fun time, and I'll say some-thing like, "Let's play talent show."

And she'll say, "Fun," and then burst into song.

Then the very next day, I might say, "Let's play talent show some more."

Only this time, she'll kind of look down at the floor and shuffle her feet. She'll say, "Ugh, I'm tired of that," or "That's boring." She won't say it meanly, and it always works out okay. But it does make me feel like maybe I did something wrong. Does that make sense? Is it possible to lose a race that you don't know you're in? Because, actually, that is what it feels like.

Anyway, all of this is a long way of saying that Chloe's word bomb gave me a long night.

Did mean people ever make you feel bad, Susan B. Anthony? People were really brutal to you. Remember that time you and your friends decided long dresses were annoying and uncomfortable and so you wore shirts and puffy pants for a year? Everywhere you went, boys and men would follow you around, laugh-ing and insulting you.

It got so bad that you finally said, "Ergh! No one is taking me seriously because of these pants. I guess I'll go back to wearing annoying and uncomfortable long dresses, even though they are the worst!"

And then there was the time you and Elizabeth Cady Stanton were "crazy" enough to believe that married women should be able to own their own property. Man, I can't even imagine what would happen if I married someone and then found out that all my stuff now belonged to them and that I couldn't own a darn thing. I'd explode! But that was the way things were back then. And when you told people that was stupid, you became the joke of America.

So how did you do it? How did you escape the word bombs that everyone threw at you? Because if I knew how to do that . . . well, then Fakey Fake's words would just bounce off me like harmless marshmallows.

Okay . . . now I really want to eat some marshmallows.

Dear Susan B. Anthony:

You know how you waited your whole life for the country to give women the right to vote? Well, I have waited my whole life to run for student council.

So—by the way—good news! Your life's work was not in vain. In 1920, fourteen years after you died, women finally got the vote. The country passed a whole constitutional amendment about it! And not just that. Women can also run for political office now—even president of the country. Maybe I will do that one day, but I also want to be a famous tap dancer/singer and run my own chain of Bundt cake stores called Susie B.'s Bundt Cakes, so we will have to see.

For now, however, I will settle for being president of Mary Routt Elementary School. And why exactly do I want to be president of Mary Routt Elementary School?

1. You get to give a campaign speech in front of everyone!

2.   If you win, you get to say the Pledge of Allegiance into a microphone at school assemblies.
3.   AND you get to be the boss of everyone.
4.   AND eternal glory.
5.   AND fairness!

It is the last of these that I want to tell you about, and I will need to share some very tragic news with you: this is a very unfair school! The usual geniuses—which is what Joselyn and I call the same five or six kids who get chosen for every single thing—always get the good stuff. And it is not because they deserve it! It's because of the teachers! The teachers act like the usual geniuses are gold and the rest of us are dumb rocks.

Take, for example, Dylan Rodriguez. Of all the usual geniuses here, Dylan Rodriguez is the most usual genius. In first grade, he was the only one of us to have a solo in the winter concert. In second grade, his Be-Kind-to-Animals-Week painting was chosen to hang in the school district office building for a whole month. In third grade, he got to represent the entire grade at the Southern California Invitational Chess Tournament—even though everyone knew that Joselyn was way better at chess than him. She just could never join the chess club because it meets after school, and as soon as class gets out, she has to take a special van to her day care. In fourth grade, Dylan had his picture in the local paper for being a really good YMCA basketball player. Plus, he got to play George Washington *and* sing Martha Washington's solo in the play about great American presidents!

Now it is fifth grade—AND WE'RE ONLY ONE MONTH INTO THE SCHOOL YEAR—but he gets to be in the Math Bowl, the Knowledge Bowl, and the Know-Your-World-History Bowl. To top it all off, this summer he was just walking through a store with his family when—out of the blue—he was asked to audition for a breakfast cereal commercial. Guess who now has his face on every box of Bitty Donut Nature Crunch? Dylan Perfect Horrible Amazing Rodriguez!

Here is the thing, Susan B. Anthony. Except for the cereal commercial, all of those other times when Dylan got to be the star, it was because of the teachers. The teachers love him. But—ha!—the teachers do not choose the student council. The students choose the student council, and so finally Joselyn and I think it will maybe be our turn to get some special attention. I am not saying that we are going to win—and I'm not saying that we *aren't* going to win. But I am saying that we will get to stand in front of everyone and give a speech, and we will get to use a big microphone, and we will get to invite our families, and we will get to show all the teachers that we are just as smart and good as the usual geniuses, and that maybe they should feel bad for not really recognizing our full potential, of which there is plenty!

But you are probably saying to yourself, "Well, that is all very interesting, Susie B., but why tell me this now? Did Mr. Springer tell you to write about your most important dreams and desires?"

No, actually. He did not assign us to write anything today because he was sick and we had a substitute who Joselyn said smelled like feet. Thankfully, I was never close enough to sniff her.

I am just writing because I want to. That is the way things are with me. Sometimes I just feel the need to write. My dad says it's because I never used to shut up when I was little. When he and my mom needed some quiet time, they would give me a notebook and say, "Shush! Please! Our brains are mush! Write all your thoughts here," and so I would. I did it even when I could only draw squiggly lines and circles. And now, when the need to write hits me, I have to get to it right away. If I don't, I will become a wiggly, useless mess.

Nothing good can come of that—just ask Lock. Once—when I couldn't find my notebook—I accidentally cut a big hole in his pillow and glued the feathers to his pillowcase so he could sleep like a chicken. I know. It doesn't make any sense, but it is a famous story that my parents like to tell.

Now we've all learned our lesson! When I feel the need to write, I am allowed to stop whatever I am doing and write, write, write, write, write.

So that is why I am writing now. I'm trying to save the world (or at least my parents, who are cleaning up the kitchen) from my wiggles.

These days, when I feel the truly crazy need to write, it is usually because something has happened. It might be something good. It might be something bad. Whatever it is, it's big.

So guess what happened today?

Today was the day my dream started to come true.

That's right! Today was the day that the student council elections were announced.

It was right after lunch, right after Joselyn and I debated which was worse, a substitute who always smelled like feet or a substitute who sometimes smelled like farts. (Farts, no question.)

We were excited because we learned that all the

fifth graders were going to a special fifth-grade-only assembly. And you know what that meant? No school-work! Oh, we were a happy bunch! We walked into that multipurpose room, and we sat on its hard, shiny floor, and we were thinking, *This is the life!*

Instantly, Principal Hodges stepped onto the stage. She did not waste any time because she never does. In her friendly but rushed voice, she told us that the time had come to elect this year's student council. She explained that serving on student council is a great honor and a serious responsibility, and that it's our chance to give back to our school and serve our community, and that she hoped everyone would consider running.

The teachers started clapping, and so all the students started clapping.

I looked at Joselyn and we smiled because we both knew that it was our turn to light up the sky.

But if anyone thought that that was all Principal Hodges had to say, they were wrong. She kept going, barely even letting the applause slow her down.

Her smile got even bigger, and she hit us with *the rules*. She liked the rules too. She said each one of them like it was something sparkly, glittery, and special.

Rule number one: we have to be in fifth grade.

Of course, we all knew that. Most of us have been at this school for over half our lives. We understand that a bunch of eight-year-olds would never be able to run this place.

Rule number two: we have to have our parents' or guardians' permission to run, especially because the student council meets every Friday at seven in the morning, and they don't want a bunch of doofuses to win and then not even show up.

I am not a doofus, but I did not know about this seven in the morning meeting business.

I looked a little uneasily at Joselyn. She knows my mom can barely get me here by eight o'clock.

But Joselyn was great. She promised that her mom would take us both if we won.

There you go! That's why you need a best spark.

Rule number three: candidates have to write a two-page, typed, double-spaced essay in a normal (not fun) font that explains why they are running for office. No late papers! None! The fifth-grade teachers, who will read the essays, won't even blink at your paper if you turn it in one second after the due date. And if the teachers decide your essay is lame or not serious—boom—no election for you!

When I heard that final rule, I sat back, stunned. I knew what was going on. If the teachers are picking the candidates, they're obviously going to pick the usual geniuses! The school was fixing the election!

I looked at Joselyn. I could tell she'd realized the same thing. But a good thing about our friendship is that we know that only one of us can freak out at a time. Since I was starting to lose it, she knew that she had to stay calm. She pressed her fingertips against my wrist and looked at me with those big brown eyes of hers. She whispered to me that it was just two pages, and that that's nothing for me.

And it's true! I could do that in my sleep!

Then she promised to remind me the day before the essay was due so that I wouldn't forget to turn it in.

My head was bobbing like crazy by this point. Yes. She would remind me, and it's not like this was just some regular homework. This was important. I wouldn't forget it if it was important.

Joselyn pressed her fingertips a little deeper into my skin. "We're winning those elections, Susie B. The teachers can't stop us. The usual geniuses can't stop us. You will be president because you love speaking into microphones, and I will be treasurer because I love to count money. This is our dream. We've been planning this forever. We've got this."

Well, thank goodness for Joselyn. Her words sparked me back up.

Dear Susan B. Anthony:

A shocking development has occurred! At dinnertime, I told my parents the exciting news that I was running for student council president. But instead of supporting me with happiness and glee, their faces turned grouchy and suspicious.

Right away, my dad asked, "How can you have a student council? You're in elementary school."

And my mom answered, "Oh, sure, they have a student council. But it doesn't do anything."

Now, here is the thing about my mom. My mom is nice, and you can tell that just by looking at her face. It's a little round, a little soft, a little wrinkled outside her eyes. She looks like she wants to be your friend. But when she wants to, she can really drill her eyeballs into a person. This was one of those times.

She started going on and on about how it's so great that I want to be involved, but that running for president sounds like a lot of work and that I'm barely keeping up with school as it is. And she couldn't let it go.

She had to drag up last week, when she kept bugging me about my homework, which had made me mad, and then me being mad had made her mad.

She said, "I'm tired of all the getting mad!"

And my dad grumped, "No one likes all the getting mad," which seemed a little unfair. He travels so much for work that he barely even hears the mad.

I told them that I would do everything by myself, that all they had to do was sign the permission slip, which would take two seconds. I said they wouldn't even have to bring me to the meetings when I won. That Joselyn's mom would take me.

Finally, Lock weighed in. He didn't sound happy for me, but he didn't sound grouchy, either. He did ask a fair question. He asked why I wanted to be president.

My goodness, Susan B. Anthony. I think your Inner Light would have shone through your whole body if you had heard the passion in my voice when I exclaimed, "It's my dream. It's been my dream forever."

Mom and Dad looked at each other and sighed. Without saying another word, they slumped back in their seats. They couldn't argue with passion. They would at least have to listen.

Lock scratched the scraggly beard he's been working on. (I personally think he should shave it off, but if I tell him that, he'll just keep it longer.) He nodded, like, *Go on, sis, blow us away!*

I explained how I would get to give a speech, say the Pledge of Allegiance into a big microphone at assemblies, have eternal glory, and beat the usual geniuses. It was pretty inspiring, if I do say so myself.

When Mom spoke again, she finally sounded like she wanted to give me some helpful advice. But guess what? She didn't even give me any advice at all! She just said that, at my age, elections are sometimes more like popularity contests.

This was literally the last thing I ever expected to hear anyone say. I mean—listen—I've been around the block. I don't get to watch a lot of movies and TV, but I've seen things. I know that popularity looks like skinny teenagers with smooth hair and expensive shoes who all clump together whenever they walk by school lockers. But my school is not like that. We don't even have lockers!

When I told them that, they asked Lock what he thought—as if he would know so much more about my own school than me.

But, aha! Finally, someone had my back! Lock was like, "I don't really remember popularity being a thing until middle school."

"Victory!" I shouted, sticking out my chest. I was right. Lock was right. Mom and Dad didn't know what the heck they were talking about.

Practically admitting as much, Mom sighed and pointed her finger at me. "Fine," she said. "But if you're going to run, you have to run for a real reason. You can't just do it to give speeches or for *eternal glory*."

Lock butted in. "In fact, never say the phrase 'eternal glory' ever again. You sound like a supervillain."

"And you can't run just to beat the usual geniuses," said Dad. "That makes you sound petty. It is petty."

"Actually," said Mom, "it makes you sound angry. People don't vote for angry women. It's a whole thing. Believe me." (And those weren't just her sort-of words. Those were her actual words.)

Something happened in that moment. Something wonderful and powerful and life-changing. I thought of you, Susan B. Anthony. I thought of you always fighting on. I pounded my fist on the table and shouted, "I will run so that I can tell people that they are being *very* unfair to angry women!"

But they didn't think that was a very convincing reason either. They said I had to stand for something that got people excited and made them feel good.

So I thought some more. I started to feel a warm,

gooey happiness inside me. Because I knew. I knew that I had to fight for something even bigger than angry women. And I knew what it was. I rose slowly from my chair and planted my hands on my hips, a vision of confidence and winningness. I said, "I will stand for all the rights of all the people all the time. Because I *do* stand for all the rights of all the people all the time!"

They all smiled at me like, *Fantastic! That's a great idea! You go, Susie B.! You are the usual genius of our whole family!*

I smiled back. Yes, I thought to myself. Yes, this is what I believe. This is what I stand for. And this is what I will talk about in a speech that will earn me eternal glory (but not in a supervillain way) and that will shame the teachers who never think about the other neglected people who never get all the good stuff that Dylan gets. And everyone will vote for me, and I will win, and Joselyn will win, and our lives will be perfect forever after.

Dear Susan B. Anthony:

Disturbing news! Get this. As usual, Joselyn was at my house yesterday so that Mom could drive us both to tap class. We were getting ready to go when Lock padded super calmly into the kitchen.

Mom was like, "What are you doing here? Aren't you supposed to be in your biology lab?"

And—big mistake—Lock said he was thinking about dropping his lab and taking it next semester.

You are probably thinking, *Well, who cares? This semester. Next semester. What's the problem?*

Get with the program, Susan B. Anthony! Lock is supposed to transfer to a university next semester! It's all Mom and Lock talk about because he was actually supposed to transfer two semesters ago, and now Mom is getting worried that he'll never transfer.

But Mom couldn't freak out the way she normally does. Joselyn was there, and Mom has a very strict rule against freaking out in front of non–family members.

Instead, Mom took her finger and tucked a strand of

hair behind her ear and said in the very sunny voice she uses to sell people houses that she thought he was set on transferring next semester.

Lock was all "um"s and "well"s and "you see"s as he tried to explain that if he takes the lab next semester, it will be the only class he has, which means he'll be able to study harder, get a better grade, and get into a better university.

But—oh, boy—that was the wrong answer.

Mom looked at him, and her face was all, *Oh, you're taking that lab, Lock! And you're taking it this semester just like you planned.*

And Lock looked at her like, *Bring it on, lady. I'm the king of the Lockdown. I know what is best for me.*

Because I am by nature a very helpful person, I chimed in, "Failure is impossible!"

Strangely, my helpfulness just seemed to make people angrier. Joselyn took a step back as Mom and Lock spun their heads toward me.

"Failure is impossible," I said again. "That was Susan B. Anthony's famous motto. It means that if you try hard, and your cause is just, good things will happen."

When no one answered, I told Lock what he always tells me. "Don't give up! You can do it."

It was quiet for a moment. Then Lock's mouth curled into a twisted smile.

I nodded encouragingly but also nervously because I had seen that twisted smile of Lock's plenty of times. It means, *Oh, you forgot that I know everything. Now you will pay!*

He clasped his hands behind his back and started pacing like a famous attorney, which is exactly what he wants to be one day.

"Don't go there," Mom told him. "She's just trying to help. You are the grown-up."

But it was too late. He was going there. It was Lockdown time! Lockdown time is when Lock proves beyond a shadow of a doubt that you don't know what you are talking about, and that you were really foolish to even try to compete with everything already locked down in his mind.

Here's how it goes:

Move number one! Make the Lockdowned person doubt themselves by turning their statement into a question.

He said, "Failure is impossible? If you try hard, and your cause is just, good things will happen?"

I mumbled something about how that was what you were always saying, Susan B. Anthony.

He nodded and moved on to Lockdown **move number two**, explaining all the ways the poor Locked and Downed must be wrong.

"So inequality exists because people don't try hard enough and not because of things like racism and sexism," he said. "Polar bears are going extinct because their cause of simply staying alive isn't just, and not because of climate change. Is that what you're saying?"

Well, that was it for Mom. She dropped her friendly house-selling voice and told us that we did not have time for an argument. She herded us into the garage, and as we got into the car, she hollered back to Lock, "And don't change the subject! This is about your bio class!"

Joselyn gave me this grimace that said, *Wow! Family drama!*

But I just shrugged because that is what it is like to have a brother who knows everything. You can't win. You can throw your seeds of so-called truth on the ground and hope they'll sprout, but most of the time Lock casts his shadows over your seeds and convinces them to shrivel up. You've just got to go with it. Anything else is too exhausting. That's what Mom says.

Unfortunately, even though she says that, she is really bad at it. She cannot go with it. Ever. She broke her own rule about not airing family business in front of non–family members. The whole way to the dance studio, she kept trying to reassure me that I shouldn't worry about Lock, that "failure is impossible" is a good motto, and that Lock was just trying to change the subject away from his bio lab.

But it was totally fine. Joselyn and I were already thinking about our tap class, which we love. Here is the great thing about tap dancing: your feet are actual musical instruments! And what could be more fun than your body having its own rhythm section?

But by now you are probably *tapping* your foot in frustration, screaming, "What the heck, Susie B.? You started this letter by very alarmingly writing 'Disturbing news.' And you even put an exclamation point at the end, which really sold the disturbingness of that phrase. What is so upsetting? Is it that Lock might not transfer next semester?"

Not really, no. I know that Lock will eventually transfer. How else will he become a famous attorney?

The problem, Susan B. Anthony, is the polar bears. As I was going to sleep, I suddenly remembered how Lock said they are going extinct because of climate change. That is not good! Polar bears are the most beautiful and majestic of all the bears. How will any of us be able to live with ourselves in a world without polar bears? How, Susan B. Anthony? How? And so now I am going to have to support the rights of all the people AND THE POLAR BEARS all the time.

"Sure," you're saying, "do that, Susie B. That sounds great and does not sound like it will be a problem for you at all."

Okay, Susan B. Anthony. But what if you were wrong and Lock is right? What if failure is possible? What if it's not just possible, but likely? I'm sure it was horrible being denied your right to vote, but you had all the time in the world to wait for women's suffrage. You could just wait, wait, wait, and even die and say, "Oh well, I'm dying now, but I know those ladies will be voting one day!" But the polar bears do not have all the time in the world. They only have as much time as there is until there are no more polar bears.

And then what?

I could not stand it. I had to get up and immediately write this letter to you on my internet-less tablet of oppression that doesn't let me stream anything.

Lock saw my light. He opened the door and asked why I wasn't sleeping.

When I explained about the bears, he rubbed the top of my head and tried to calm me down, saying that stressing about polar bears is not helping any polar bears.

And when I told him I could not calm down because maybe he is right and failure is possible, this regretful look sparkled in his eyes. Then he basically said what Mom had said. That he'd just been trying to change the subject.

But I didn't even see why that mattered. If polar bears might go extinct, they might go extinct.

He took my tablet and turned it off. "Little sis, it is true that failure is possible. Bad things happen to people—and polar bears—who don't deserve it. But . . . that is why we fight on, right?" (Or, well, it was something like that. I'm pretty tired. For sure, he said the fighting on part.)

I wasn't sure if I believed him. I mean, on the one hand, some of my first memories are about Mom taking me and Lock to protests and rallies on behalf of, well, all the rights of all the people. But did they make a difference? Did they matter? Or wasn't it always like this? Something bad happened. We protested with hundreds of people. Everything calmed down for a while. And then everything started over again.

How could the polar bears afford that kind of merry-go-round?

Finally, Lock convinced me to go back to bed. So I am going back to bed. But here is the question Lock never answered: What's going to happen to those polar bears? If hundreds of people coming together can't save them, how can one Susie B. do anything?

Dear Susan B. Anthony:

Okay. I know you've probably been worrying about me since my last letter ended on a sad note. But it's okay now! My answer came to me when I was writing my two-page essay about why I was running for student council president. I was very specifically *not* mentioning the usual geniuses. And—although it annoyed me—I was trying hard not to sound angry as I explained how, as president, I would support all the rights of all the people and, now, polar bears. I would support the rights to equality, and to being appreciated for who you are, and to no bullies, and to enough food and housing for everyone, and to eating at least *some* sugary snacks sometimes and watching *some* TV shows and playing *some* video games, and just, really, all the rights—especially the polar bears' rights to enough ice and glaciers and polar bear food.

And that's when I had my big brain breakthrough. *Polar bear rights!* That's how I will fight on for the polar bears! As student council president! I won't just use the big and beautiful microphone to lead kids in the Pledge of Allegiance! I will use the big and beautiful microphone to give speeches about how we have to save the polar bears. And people will love my speeches because who wouldn't love speeches like that?

Everyone will say, "There's Susie B. She's fighting for polar bears!" And my speeches will make them care about the polar bears, and if we all care, they'll be saved! Right?

Of course they will! I made the speeches a big part of my passionate and inspiring two-page essay. As I bet you would guess, it was some of my most poetic writing ever.

Now, a real amateurish kid would finish their essay and turn it in the very next day. But I have learned through years of experience that the secret to good writing is stepping away. That's right. You have to take what you wrote and then abandon it for as long as possible so that when you come back to it, you will see it with a stranger's eyes. Only when you've seen things with a stranger's eyes can you make what you wrote even better, because only then can you realize that what you thought was *really* good was actually only *pretty* good.

So, because I will not give those fifth-grade teachers any possible excuse to reject my candidacy, I waited until the final day to turn in my running-for-student-council paperwork. And, boy, it was a good thing that I waited. When I reread my work the night before it was due, I realized that I could be way more inspiring! I added even more stuff about how polar bears have the right to not go extinct and how anyone who doesn't want to save the polar bears is horrible. By the time I was done fixing it all up, I was almost crying! My writing was that sad and beautiful. Personally, I don't see how anyone could read what I wrote and not cry. In fact, if those fifth-grade teachers do not at least mist up when reading the part about the polar bears, there is definitely something wrong with them, and they should probably be banned from any of the helping professions.

To be honest, my revised essay did go over the two-page requirement by a couple (or six) pages. But here is one thing that was unclear: Were we supposed to write *at least* two pages or *no more than* two pages? In my opinion, if we need to prove that we are taking this election seriously, then the *at least* two pages answer makes more sense. Don't you agree?

I'm worried that maybe you don't agree. I'm worried that you are one of those people who likes to remind me that I don't always pay attention to details. And it's true! I don't! Especially when I'm excited! But I forgot that I was like that until this morning. By that time, it was too late to change what I'd written. So then I just kept wondering: Will it be okay that my two-page essay is actually eight pages? Will the teachers reject me because of that? Will they be so tied to rules that they will be unable to see how poetic and amazing my essay is?

Of course, this was the one day of the year that my mom was actually running on time. I got to school early, which meant that I couldn't even get Joselyn's opinion because she wasn't there yet.

I did the only thing I could. I waited for Joselyn by the drop-off lane.

Technically, we are not allowed to wait by the drop-off lane. I guess the school thinks some kid will jump into a distracted driver's car as it pulls away, although—think it through, school—kids are smarter than that.

The point is, as soon as we are dropped off, we are supposed to go to our lines, which are painted on the blacktop. Every class has a line, from kinders through fifth graders. And we are supposed to stay in our lines until our teachers come and escort us to class.

But I really needed Joselyn to calm me down and tell me that everything would be okay. I bent down and kept pretending to tie my shoelace while I actually spied on the arriving cars.

Here is a surprise! It turns out that taking forever to pretend-tie your shoes can draw a lot of attention to a person.

First, Carson, my desk partner and old friend from reading lab, walked by and asked what I was doing.

I told him I was tying my shoe.

"No, you're not." He crouched down next to me and pretended to tie his own shoelaces. "What's the deal? What's the situation? What's the plan? What's the what the?"

Yeah. That's Carson for you. He can be a bit much for some people, but I get Carson because of his butterfly brain. Plus, he is nice and is also a very good artist— like *professional* good—which I respect because I can barely draw stick-figure people.

The point is, I didn't want to be mean, but I didn't need a lot of attention focused on me either.

I told him it wasn't a big deal.

But he didn't get up. He just stayed there pretending to tie *his* shoe!

Then perfect Dylan Rodriguez walked by. He stopped, turned around, and came back. He watched us for a minute.

I was thinking, *Move it, Mr. Wonderful. I'm trying to blend in.*

And he was like, "Why are you guys pretending to tie your shoes?"

Carson looked up at him and winked one set of his extra-long eyelashes. He said, "Hush, hush, eye to eye"—which I don't even know what that means—"it's a secret, big secret. I can't tell you."

Then Dylan Rodriguez bent down and pretended to tie *his* shoe. "What kind of secret?" He asked like he really wanted to know, which just proves that one person's usual genius is another person's gossip sniffer.

All of a sudden, Soozee Gupta huddled down next to us too. "Hi," she said. She was sucking on a lollipop and wearing a very fashionable purple hat that sent the message, *I'm stylish and hip. I spell my name in a fascinating and creative way.*

In the bubbly and happy tone that only Soozee can pull off, she began telling us how she was starting a new lunchtime club.

Even though my face was shadowed by me pretending to tie my shoes, I had to very dramatically roll my eyes. Soozee is always starting lunchtime clubs. There was the Olympics Club, the Chips and Salsa Club, the Rescue Dog Club. And those are just the ones that I can remember off the top of my head. She invites everyone, but it's always just the same three or four kids that ever come, and usually, after a few weeks, even those kids are ready to move on to something else.

This time, she's starting an Emergency Preparedness Club that will be all about what to do in different emergencies. Interestingly, she did share a fun tidbit with us as we were fiddling with our laces. She said you should always keep a stash of lollipops and granola bars in your car. They won't melt. They last almost forever. And who knows? One day, you might be hungry and trapped in your car after an earthquake, snowstorm, or major disaster, and then you'll be glad because as least you won't starve.

Obviously, my first thought was that my parents are dropping the ball when it comes to thinking about these things. In our trunk, we only keep grocery store bags and big packages of toilet paper that my mom always forgets to bring into the house.

For a second, I considered going to Soozee's club because—duh—if my parents don't know about preparing our car for an emergency . . . what else don't they know about? But Joselyn thinks Soozee's clubs are a little weird. So—no offense to Soozee—but of course I have to choose Joselyn over her.

Soozee unzipped her backpack and pulled out a handful of lollipops. They were for the club members, which suddenly made the club seem even more worth checking out. But in total Soozee fashion, she didn't even say you had to go to her club to get one. She just handed one to each of us.

I think they were meant for our cars, but Carson instantly tore the wrapper off his, and when Soozee didn't seem to mind, I did the same thing because it was just a little bit of candy and not a giant chocolate Santa. I didn't think I would go completely berserk or anything.

Only perfect Dylan Rodriguez took his and put it in his backpack.

But that's the usual geniuses for you. If they are not kicking you in the shins with their winningness, they are shaming you with their willpower.

Another kid came by. But this kid didn't crouch down next to us. This kid hovered over us. She was wearing expensive boots, the kind my mom says no kid should have since they cost more than actual grown-up shoes.

I'll give you one guess who that was.

That's right! Old Fakey Fake. I knew right away that she was going to be tricky with her meanness this time. Everyone knows that she is in love with Dylan

Rodriguez, and so when he's around, she's 😽😹😽😻.

She is always, "Oh, Dylan, you look so good today," and "Oh, Dylan, you are so amazing," and "Oh, Dylan, do you like my hair/dress/picture/gigantic mass of fakeness?"

But we also all know that he is not in love with her. Whenever she starts talking to him, he makes up some excuse and sprints away. And that is what happened this time. As soon as he realized it was Chloe lording herself over us, he said, "I guess I should get to my line." And off he went.

Carson—who is way smarter than most people give him credit for—followed right behind Dylan, which left just me, Soozee, and Old Fakey Fake.

Her voice as sweet as syrup, Chloe said, "Hey, Susie Bumblebee"—which we both know is not my name. Then she asked if I needed help with my shoes.

At first, I thought she was trying to make Soozee wonder if I could actually tie my shoes, because then Soozee was all, "Oh! Do you need help?"

But that wasn't it at all! That was just her setup so she could get the principal involved. That's right! She was trying to get me in trouble!

She waved at Principal Hodges, who was standing by the drop-off lane. "Principal Hodges!" she shouted. "I think Susie B. needs help. Otherwise, I'm sure she would go to her line. I'm sure she is not up to *mischief* or anything." She actually said that! About the mischief! Really!

Principal Hodges started walking right to us, but luckily, her shoes were making it hard for her. Normally, Principal Hodges wears what my mom calls "sensible shoes," which are more Susie than Soozee, if you know what I mean. My mom is a big fan of sensible shoes because she says two decades of ballet ruined her feet and that anyone who wears uncomfortable footwear is a big sucker.

You would guess that a no-nonsense person like Principal Hodges would think the same thing, but today she had on very high heels and a very worried expression. I think she was either thinking, *Oh, no! I think I'm going to kill myself in these shoes!* or *Oh, no! That Susie B. is up to terrible mischief!* It was hard to tell.

I didn't want to take any chances—not on such an important day. I superfast stood up and yelled that I was just tying my shoe and not doing anything bad.

Principal Hodges nodded. Then she pointed us to the blacktop, looking very relieved that she didn't have to walk any farther in those shoes.

Fakey Fake was smiling all innocently at Principal Hodges, but I saw the sneakiness in her eyes as she turned around and ran to our class line, completely ignoring Soozee, who was following behind her yelling, "Hey, Chloe, did you hear about my club?"

I looked one last time over at the drop-off lane, and—thank goodness—there was Joselyn, stepping out of her car.

I checked to make sure Principal Hodges wasn't watching anymore, and then I ran to Joselyn, saying, "Ack! Emergency!"

We walked toward our line as I explained how long my essay had become. When I was done, I asked if she agreed that it was most likely okay to write more than two pages since that would probably just impress the teachers even more.

But Joselyn didn't think it was okay! She reminded me that teachers are natural-born sticklers who love rules almost as much as they love usual geniuses!

I was starting to panic. I asked, "Do you think it's *bad* that I wrote more than two pages?"

"Yes!" she said, twisting her head back and forth and gnashing her teeth. Seriously! She actually gnashed her teeth, Susan B. Anthony, just like in books! I did not believe that I would ever in my life see real teeth gnashing, but she was gnashing so much that her gums sparkled in the sunshine.

Our classmates began to walk single file behind Mr. Springer to our class. Without another word, we ran to catch up.

Oh, I was feeling stressed. Let me tell you something. It is one thing when you think someone else might crush your dreams. It is another thing when you think you've been stupid enough to crush them yourself.

Once we were in the classroom, I dropped into my chair and banged my head against the desktop, my wonderful, inspiring, too-long, poetic essay still clutched in my hand.

Carson dropped his head on the desk too. He turned toward me so that his cheek lay flat on the wood-grained surface. His eyes tried to catch mine from my tunnel of forehead-on-desk darkness. For no reason at all, he started making a chicken sound. "Bock, bock, bock, bock, bock."

When I didn't move or say anything, he went, "Gobble, gobble, gobble, gobble, gobble." Then, "Quack, quack, quack, quack, quack."

When I still didn't move or say anything, he sniffed, then said, "What's wrong?" And he didn't say it like he was joking around. He said it like he meant it.

Mr. Springer and most of the kids in class were still getting settled, so I turned my cheek toward him and started yakking.

Now, you have to remember that Carson's brain is even more butterflyish than mine. He is such a wiggle monkey that he has a whole pile of fidget spinners in his desk. He even has permission to chew Big Red gum in class because spicy cinnamon gum helps him focus. So I was very grateful that Carson was as still as could be as I told him the tragic story of how I'd probably destroyed my own dreams by writing too long of a really good essay.

"Now the teachers will for sure reject my candidacy," I said. "You know how they are always looking for ways to support the usual geniuses."

"The usual geniuses," said Carson, practically gagging in disgust. Carson hates the usual geniuses even more than I do. In fact, Carson invented the saying "usual genius." Joselyn and I just stole it without even asking. And if you think I hate all the teachers focusing on the usual geniuses, it's nothing compared to how much Carson hates it. That's because Carson doesn't just have a butterfly brain like me. He also has this thing called dyslexia, which is a very fancy (and so I think kind of fun) word that means he has a hard time with reading.

Just to remind you, Susan B. Anthony, there is nothing wrong with that! Brains are different! That's a fact! And I will not have you thinking that Carson isn't smart just because he is not an expert reader like me!

Smarts are different too! Like I told you already, Carson is really smart at art. He will probably grow up to be as famous as the painter Pablo Picasso, who Carson happens to be doing his Hero Project on. Carson is so good an artist that he can draw things like flying cars in five seconds flat. He does it all the time.

You are probably thinking, *Well, you have convinced me, Susie B. That boys sounds like he has better art smarts than anyone in your class!*

He does! In fact, I think that he is more than a *usual* genius. He is an *unusual* genius!

But here is the problem. He is always getting in trouble for his unusual genius because he is always accidentally doing art instead of schoolwork.

You are wondering, *Can't you just tell him to wait and do his art genius stuff during art time?*

Sure! Easy peasy! Except guess what? We have art once a week from one to two o'clock. It is a very big deal because lots of schools have no art time at all. Of course, we are always excited about it, and we know that we are really lucky. All of us are lucky, that is, except for Carson. Good news for the usual geniuses: Guess when Carson has reading lab? Every day from one to two o'clock. So the only time we actually have art is the only time Carson is not even in the classroom.

"That's not fair," I can practically hear you moaning. "Why would the school pull Carson from class during the one time when he can super-brightly shine?"

I'll tell you! It's because the school says art is extra. Since it's extra, they say it's more important that Carson go to reading lab than that he does the one thing he loves.

So—duh—because Carson can never do the class's weekly art projects, guess whose art always gets hung on the wall or in the principal's office or anyplace special?

That's right! The usual geniuses! Just last week we had an art activity connected to our Hero Project. This woman came in and taught us about cubism, which is a whole style of art where things that are not cubes are made to look a little like cubes, or parts of cubes. Once we learned about it, we were supposed to make cubist portraits of our heroes. The one I made of you looked something like this:

Not too bad, right? True, it's not too good, either, but I never said that I was the art genius.

Do you know who else is not an art genius? Dylan Rodriguez! And yet it is Dylan Rodriguez's charcoal drawing of this computer guy named Steve Jobs that is hanging in front of the whiteboard. The rest of us were "invited" to take our portraits home! And, while I don't remember it perfectly, I'm pretty sure the portrait Dylan Rodriguez made looked like this:

When Carson came back from reading lab, he took one look at Dylan's picture and rolled his eyes right past the top of his head. He nodded toward the whiteboard and asked whose it was.

I didn't even have to tell him. I just rolled my eyeballs up even higher than he had. "Yours would have been better," I told him, which just meant that I was saying the plain truth.

He said, "You know who the best cubist artist of all time was? Pablo Picasso."

I couldn't believe it. Remember? That's Carson's Hero Project guy! His own Hero Project guy was the king of cubism, and Carson didn't even get to draw him.

Oh, it just made me dislike the usual geniuses even more.

But that was then. Now—because of my too-long amazing essay—it was my turn to be depressed and sad about the unfairness of life. And that meant it was Carson's turn to be encouraging for me.

When I moaned and dropped my eight-page essay on the floor like the reject garbage that it was, he got right down and picked it up. He said, "You can't give up now. You wrote the darn thing. At least turn it in."

He shouted across the room to Mr. Springer.

Mr. Springer looked up from taking roll and tried to hide the classic frown and scrunched eyebrows of an interrupted teacher. He cleared his throat and asked Carson what he wanted.

Still shouting, Carson asked the big question. Would the fifth-grade teachers read my essay even if it was longer than two pages?

The whole class grew quiet. Everyone turned and stared at me in disbelief. In disbelief, I tell you! Like they couldn't believe I was even trying to run, that I even thought I could possibly win!

I swallowed and glanced at Joselyn, whose desk is right by Mr. Springer's. Her shoulders were hunched, her chin low. It looked like she was wondering the same thing, like maybe people wouldn't consider her student council material either.

Mr. Springer stood up from his desk. He pointed at my essay, where it sat crinkled on my desk, and said in his froggy voice, "Of course we'll read it. Bring it here. I'm excited to read what you wrote."

Carson plopped back down in his chair and boomed, "Go, Susie B.!"

And that gave me the boost of bravery I needed to walk over and hand my paper to Mr. Springer.

Mr. Springer started to flip through it. At first, he looked surprised, and then a little impressed when he realized just how much I had written. He stopped on one of the pages and scratched his stubbly chin in the way he always does when he is thinking about something.

I knew just the words that were spinning around in that big head of his. He was thinking, *I have made a big mistake in not lumping Susie B. together with the other usual geniuses. What a bozo I've been!*

But then he surprised me by saying, "Polar bears?" And he asked if I understood what the student council president actually did.

"Of course," I said. "That's why I'm running." I puffed out my chest in a very confident way, but secretly, I was thinking that I should probably actually look into what the president does. That would be a good thing to know.

Then—unbelievably—he told me the president doesn't get to go around and give lots of speeches about whatever they want and that they can't really do much about polar bears.

I glanced back at my classmates. How had I missed it? Mr. Springer was already turning them against me! I said loudly and with great friendliness, "I have a whole plan, Mr. Springer. I will support all the rights of all the people and polar bears. You'll see." I spread my hands wide, and my voice turned serious. "Polar bears could go extinct, and we have to put a stop to that."

Well, ha-ha-hoodly-who! I got a few impressed raised eyebrows for that one!

But no sooner was I delighting in those eyebrows than Dylan walked up and said that he had paperwork to turn in too.

"What kind of paperwork?" I asked, even though

I knew *exactly* what kind of paperwork it was. It was running-for-student-council-president paperwork.

But did Dylan Rodriguez even bother to look at me when he answered? No! Turning his can't-even-have-crooked-teeth smile on Mr. Springer, he said, "I'm applying to run for student council president." And he was very ho-hum about it too, like, *Of course I am running! Didn't we all know this would happen? Aren't I the savior of everything and everyone?*

Mr. Springer started smiling and congratulating Dylan like he'd already won. Then my teacher—who you would hope would be fair to everyone—flipped through Dylan's three pages and nodded, like, *Oh, this looks perfect because perfect Dylan turned it in.*

"Well, good luck," I said, all la-di-da pleasantly, because I did not want either of them to see how upsetting the news of Dylan's candidacy was to me.

As I was walking to my seat, I began to feel a little tickle in my brain, a little I-think-I've-forgotten-something-important tickle. And that tickle kept getting ticklier and ticklier until I had to stop right in place, press my fingers against my scalp, and mutter in front of everyone, "What are you forgetting, Susie B.?"

"You're forgetting to think with your mouth closed," smirked Old Fakey Fake.

Maturely ignoring her, I continued on to my seat. But when I sat down—kaboom—it hit me. The first page of Dylan's paperwork was his permission slip! I was so worried about my essay that I completely forgot my stupid permission slip. Agggh! My butterfly brain had sunk me again.

Dear Susan B. Anthony:

Today we are supposed to write about our families, and I am not supposed to get offtrack. I am only supposed to write two paragraphs because while Mr. Springer likes my enthusiasm, he says he does not want to feel his life force drain slowly from his body, which he says happens when there is too much grading to do.

I am supposed to write one paragraph about how your family inspired you to become the hero you were, and then I am supposed to write one paragraph about how my family inspired me to be the person I am. And my paragraphs are supposed to have five sentences because fifth graders write paragraphs with five sentences, and fourth graders write paragraphs with four sentences, and third graders write paragraphs with three sentences. And each paragraph should have a topic sentence and a concluding sentence. And those should count as two of the five sentences.

Your family inspired you to be a big protester. They

were always protesting injustice, and that made you always want to protest injustice too. Your family especially believed in protesting against slavery, to which I say, "Amen to that, sister!" Lock says slavery is America's original sin and that we still haven't dealt with all of its consequences. So I am glad that you were on the right side of history there.

Something in my family that really inspires me is Lock. As you have probably guessed, he hates injustice too. In kindergarten, he kicked a kid who said that only boys could use the tricycles. He got sent to the principal and everything, but he didn't get in trouble. In fact, the lady who was principal back then told him that she wished all kids cared about fairness as much as he did. It's one of Mom's favorite stories about Lock. She tells it all the time, except she usually leaves out the part where the principal said that he couldn't go around kicking people, and he answered, "I'll just bite them instead." But don't worry, Susan B. Anthony. These days all Lock bites are veggie burgers, and that's because last week he became a vegan, even though my parents say that if he expects them to stop cooking bacon, he's got another thing coming.

Of course, my favorite thing about Lock is that he always encourages me. When I was having a hard time learning to read, he would tell me to keep trying, and when I am feeling especially mad that I've never seen a Star Wars movie, he tells me there are more important things to feel mad about, and if I am worried—like I was about the polar bears—he always tells me to calm the heck down. In fact, just recently he had to do that again.

Remember the other day when I forgot my running-for-student-council permission slip? I called Lock right away from Carson's phone. I explained that I was freaking out, and that I needed my permission slip, and that Dylan Rodriguez was running for president, and that he will probably win because he always wins, and that I thought this time it would be different, and that my essay was eight pages, and that Mr. Springer totally wants me to lose. Believe me, it was a miracle he could keep up with what I was saying. My mouth was moving a mile a minute.

He cut me right off and told me to calm down.

I said I didn't want to calm down.

But he told me I needed to calm down immediately.

I took a deep breath, and then another. I said, "Okay. I'm calmed down."

He paused a beat and told me it was no big deal. He would drop the permission slip off on his way to class.

Wow. It was like he had lifted a giant boulder off my chest. I felt so much better. But that is why Lock is so great. He is always just, "Whatever. We'll figure it out." And everybody needs someone like that in their life.

Sadly, before I could thank Lock, Carson grabbed his phone away from me and motioned toward Mr. Springer, who was turning around from the whiteboard to face the class.

It had been a close one! Bringing out a phone during school is an instant trip to Principal Hodges. I had buried myself under my sweatshirt and halfway under my desk, but Mr. Springer has an eye for these things. If he had found me talking on Carson's phone? Listen, it would have been bad for both of us.

I gave Carson my most grateful smile, and he shrugged like it was no big deal. But we both knew that it was a big deal. For sure, I owed him a favor.

At lunchtime Joselyn and I went to the front office to see if Lock had come by. Not only was my permission slip there, but so was a cupcake with a tiny flag on it. On the flag, Lock had written, "Vote for Susie!" So, yeah, of course he inspires me!

And I am feeling much better about everything now because my mom reminded me that "failure is impossible." She also said losing isn't failing. Not taking chances is failing. So—ack!—I guess we will just have to wait and see if the teachers will be fair and recognize my essay for the great piece of writing that it is.

Dear Susan B. Anthony:

First five-sentence paragraph:

This topic sentence is about a challenge you faced when you were a child. When you were a kid, you wanted to learn long division, but this teacher guy told you that girls weren't smart enough to do that. The truth was that he did not know how to do long division himself. He straight out lied to you! I will conclude this paragraph by telling you that that teacher guy was a jerk.

Second five-sentence paragraph:

This topic sentence is telling you how you responded to your challenge. You went to this farmhand you knew and were all, "Dude, teach me long division because of course I can do math just as good as any boy." And that guy was all, "Totally." And he taught you. So that was how you learned long division, and with that I will conclude this paragraph.

Dear Susan B. Anthony:

This is not a topic sentence that says that it is a topic sentence. That is because you do not need to identify your topic sentence with the words "topic sentence." The topic sentenceness of a topic sentence is implied because paragraphs are supposed to be organic. Like fruit! And I do not need to take Mr. Springer's paragraph-writing corrections so literally, but I do need to follow the directions.

Speaking of fruit, I am very fond of mangoes, and I am supposed to tell you that because that is the writing prompt for the day, and it is related to our unit on nutrition. What was your favorite fruit? I bet it was apples. You just seem like you were an apple kind of gal. And I don't need to say that this is a concluding sentence because that is also just implied.

PS: Dylan just told Mr. Springer that his favorite fruit is a tomato. Ha! How Dylan Rodriguez is that? I didn't even know tomatoes *were* fruits. I had to look it up. But it's true! A tomato is a stinking fruit! Do you know what I say to that? "No, sir! NO! Unacceptable!" But yeah. That's the guy who wants to lead us! Mr. Tomatohead.

Dear Susan:

Can I call you plain Susan? It seems like we have been doing this for a while now and that we should just be casual with each other.

Good news! This is not an official journal entry. I do not have to follow anyone's rules about paragraph writing, and I would like to say that I think rules about paragraph writing are lame. I have read paragraphs that are one word long, and I have read paragraphs that are a page long. I do not believe this business about fifth graders having to write five-sentence-long paragraphs. I believe this business of students having to write paragraphs with as many sentences as they have grades sounds like teacher-made-up silliness. But why, Susan? Why have such silliness? It makes no sense at all.

All I know is that if I am elected student council president, I will put a stop to it. I will tell the teachers, "Enough! Freedom for paragraph writers! Let us write what we want!"

Dear Susan:

This is not an official journal entry either, so don't worry. It won't be boring, boring, boring five-sentence-paragraph slogs of boringness.

Instead, I have shocking information!

Yesterday, Carson and I were doing Hero Project math. That is not the shocking part. I'm just setting the scene. We had to figure out how long it would have taken our heroes to travel different places using different types of transportation. (If your train never stopped and moved at a constant rate of thirty-five miles per hour, it would have taken you close to four days to travel from Rochester, New York, to Portland, Oregon, where you went to give a speech in 1905. By the way, you were eighty-five at the time! Way to go for being active in your old age. We are always trying to get my great-grandma to take an exercise class or get a cat or something. But she says she is happy puttering around her house and that she is a grown woman and we should mind our own business.)

Anyway, I happened to mention my suspicions about five-sentence-long paragraphs being teacher-made-up silliness to Carson.

He was very fascinated and said that he would ask his mom. She is a school principal in Pasadena.

Well, today at lunch, Joselyn and I were chatting away when Carson came over and joined us. (This isn't the shocking part either! Hold your horses!) Right away, Old Fakey Fake looked over at us from her table. She scrunched up her beady eyes and started whispering to the three Rs, probably saying something like, "Oh, look, the butterfly brains must be in love. Kissy, kissy, smoochy, smoochy."

And the three Rs giggled and laughed, and I could tell they were not laughing in an *Isn't the world a beautiful place and aren't we lucky to live in it?* way. No, they were laughing in a *Ha! We are better than you* way.

Now, listen. Don't give me any of this "Oh, come on! It's the twenty-first century! Everyone knows that boys and girls can just be friends" stuff that my parents gave me when I told them this story.

I know it is the twenty-first century, and I know boys and girls can be friends. Duh. But I also know that not everyone really believes that. Every day, I see boys believing boys have to be one way, and girls believing girls have to be another way.

Just last year, Old Fakey Fake wrote a poem saying girls like to wear "their best dresses" on Thanksgiving. Luckily, she is not a usual genius, so it was not hung on the Wall of Usual-Genius-Tribute, but she did read her poem aloud. I heard it. And—bam—as soon as the words came out of her mouth, I knew that I needed to wear pants to Thanksgiving dinner at my grand-parents' house. It was disappointing, too. I had really wanted to wear the green dress that makes my eyes look bluish-green, which is so much more mysterious and conversation-starting than bluish-gray.

Of course, I didn't care that Old Fakey Fake directed her gossipy face toward our lunch table. But Joselyn is more sensitive about these things, especially—sometimes—lately. Her opinion is, "Hey! Let's make people think we're like everyone else," while my opin-ion is, "Wait. Are we ever *not* like everyone else?"

Anyway, you gotta keep your best spark happy when you can, so I was polite, but not all "Welcome! Join us! I'm so happy to see you!"

"Cookie cutters," said Carson, planting his elbows on the table and giving us a big wink.

Joselyn pulled back, seeming a little worried that Carson was going to go all winky-yelly-wacky on us.

I pushed my hair away from my face so that every-one could see that I—Susie B.—was not afraid of Old

Fakey Fake. Loudly, I told him to explain what he was talking about.

Carson looked around like he was a spy checking for other spies. He leaned forward and said the craziest thing. He said teachers treat paragraphs like cookie cutters, and that as kids get older, the teachers ask them to make the cookie cutter bigger, but they don't want to change the shape of the cookie cutter. They want the shape to always stay the same, the shape being a topic sentence, a certain number of sentences about the topic sentence, and a concluding sentence. His mom told him.

That just didn't make any sense to me. In books, some paragraphs are like that, but some aren't. I mean . . . I guess paragraphs are always . . . like . . . maybe about one big idea? But they definitely aren't cookie cutters.

I asked Carson why the heck teachers would do that.

His eyes took on a weird brightness, and I knew that he was about to spill a truth bomb that would change our lives forever. (Pay attention, Susan B. Anthony! This is the shocking part!)

He said, "It's because the teachers are *afraid*."

Joselyn's eyes crinkled right up. She couldn't believe it.

Oh, but he wasn't done. He was just warming up. He

was getting ready to blow our minds. He said, "Teachers are afraid of paragraphs *because they don't actually understand them themselves.*"

I swear, the look on my face must have been something else, like maybe I'd seen an alien just walk off a spaceship or something. How could teachers not understand paragraphs? They teach them!

But that's what his mom told him! She said that since some teachers don't really understand paragraphs themselves, they turn them into one unbreakable rule. That way they don't have to admit the truth. And this is the truth: no one really understands paragraphs. Paragraphs are one of the great mysteries of the universe!

Joselyn still seemed unconvinced. She turned her body away from Carson like he wasn't even there.

But I believed him! "Oh my gosh!" I yelled, and suddenly it wasn't just Fakey Fake's table that was staring at us. It was every table. Even the people at Soozee's Emergency Preparedness table stared at us—and it was a wonder they could hear at all since they were wrapping one another's heads in gauze.

We waited for everyone to return to their own conversations. Then I said, "This is just like Susan B. Anthony!"

Now it was Carson's turn to look at me like I was going to say something incredible.

So I told him and Joselyn the story of how that sexist doofus guy told you, Susan, that girls couldn't learn long division, when he just didn't know how to do it himself. He was afraid to admit what he didn't understand about math, just like some teachers are afraid to admit what they don't understand about paragraphs!

Finally, Joselyn seemed to see the light. She was clenching her teeth like, "ERRRGH! Grown-ups!"

But then Carson told a story about his hero, Pablo Picasso, and how he came to believe that the best artists have to break the rules.

Carson is always way more relaxed when he is talking about art, so he didn't seem so amped up. Whether it was that, or just what he was saying, Joselyn inched closer. She bent her head toward Carson so she could really listen, and she nodded along as he explained how Pablo, who was from Spain, had dyslexia. Just like Carson! And because he had a hard time learning to read, some people treated Pablo like he wasn't smart.

But Pablo's dad said, "I'm putting you in art school."

Obviously, that was a genius move. Eventually, Pablo broke all the art rules and became super famous. Carson says he changed art forever.

Can you imagine? He changed art FOREVER! Like, in a thousand years, when people are living on Mars, art will still be different because of Pablo Picasso.

I said that you would have probably really liked Pablo, Susan, especially since you both liked smashing rules so much.

And then Joselyn said her hero also liked smashing rules.

Now, I had known that Joselyn was doing her project on this millionaire lady named Madam C. J. Walker, but I had not known until then that Madam C. J. Walker was the first *self-made* woman millionaire in the whole country. And get this! She was African American! She made all her money selling beauty products.

Your lives overlapped, Susan B. Anthony!

I wonder if you two actually knew each other. I tried looking it up on the internet, but there wasn't anything about it.

I bet you did know her. I bet you were friends and admirers. I bet when you saw each other, you cheered, "Go, fellow fighter for women! Go!"

I bet she said to you, "Everyone told me, 'You can't be a business lady. You can't be a millionaire. You are a measly female—and a Black measly female at that.' But I told them, 'Um, excuse you. I will be a millionaire.

I will be awesome. You can't stop me, and all you haters can go jump in a lake, where I will smile at you from my big ol' yacht.'"

And then I bet she said, "Let's go hang out on my boat, Susan B. Anthony."

And you guys cruised all around, and if people said racist and sexist things to you, you just yelled, "In your faces, suckers! And we will even wear pants if we want to!"

Anyway—the point is—it turned out that me, Joselyn, and Carson had a very interesting conversation! And now we might all go to the Norton Simon Museum in Pasadena together. There are actual paintings by Pablo Picasso there, and since Carson and his mom are museum members, they can get me and Joselyn in for free.

But here is the big takeaway, Susan B. Anthony: teachers are afraid of things, just like kids are afraid of things, and we should be nice about it because . . . well, just because. But, at the same time, I still say Freedom for Paragraph Writers! Don't take your fears out on us, teachers! Short paragraphs. Long paragraphs. Let the paragraphs be! And get it together! If you want to be afraid of something, choose something big, like the end of polar bears.

You know what I've been thinking? If polar bears go extinct, how long would it take until some jerks began to say that they never actually existed, that they were just some internet fake, just like the people who say dinosaurs were fake?

Let me tell you something. If that happens, I will spend my whole life stomping out that lie! I will convince everyone that—once upon a time—there were these big white bears who lived in the Arctic and were super beautiful and strong. I will make that my job, even if that means giving up my dreams of being a famous tap dancer/singer, running a chain of Bundt cake shops, and maybe even being president of the United States. But I shouldn't have to do that, and I won't have to do that if the world can just save the polar bears! And when I am president of Mary Routt Elementary School—one way or another—we will at least try!

Dear Susan:

Big news!

This morning, at school, I saw all these kids—including Joselyn—standing near the front office. I ran to check it out, and guess what? They were looking at the list of people who get to run for student council! The office people had hung it right outside the office door, and everybody was staring at it with eyes that said, "Wow! These kids wrote amazing essays that the fifth-grade teachers loved. I'm so jealous!"

I won't bore you with the names of people running for vice president and secretary. Who the heck cares about them? They're nobody I know. But I will tell you that Joselyn (good news) gets to run for treasurer. Of course, this is no surprise. She is the kind of person who never forgets permission slips, or writes too-long essays, or even procrastinates over anything since her motto is "Ack! Procrastinating is too stressful!"

She is running against some kid named Matt Chan. Like Soozee, he is in Ms. Zamorano's class. He is also a friend of Dylan's. He is not a usual genius (more good news). But he is the next worst thing. He is super athletic (bad news). We've seen him playing soccer at lunch. He is not as good as Dylan, mind you, who LOVES soccer, but he is solidly good. And Carson told me that Matt is one of the best swimmers on his swim team. He even wins in races where he has to do the butterfly stroke, which everyone knows is the most impossible stroke in the world.

I do not know how things were in your day, Susan, but these days, being super athletic earns a kid respect and even a bit of school-wide celebrity. Obviously, Joselyn is worried.

Matt, on the other hand, does not seem worried at all. We saw him looking at the list of candidates. He had a big, smug grin on his face, as if to say, "I am not at all worried about winning because boys who are good at sports are totally at the top of the food chain."

But, Susan B. Anthony, as much as you are sympathizing with poor Joselyn, you are probably dying to know about me, since I am the one who is writing to you all the time. And (good news) I made the cut! My name was listed right under the words "Candidates for Student Council President."

Okay. In all honesty, I bet you were expecting this.

Let's face it, my eight-page essay must have been pretty fantastic reading for the fifth-grade teachers.

They probably said to Mr. Springer, "Oh my gosh, I hope your student Susie B. wins this election! Her beautiful writing about supporting all the rights of all the people and polar bears made me cry!"

And I bet Mr. Springer answered, "Wow! I am truly shocked. All this time, I have been going along with everyone else and thinking that Dylan Rodriguez is the most amazing fifth grader in all of history, when, in fact, I have not noticed that Susie B. is not even afraid of the universal mystery of paragraphs. She would probably be the best student council president this school has ever had!"

Of course—bad news—Dylan was also approved to run for president. He was too perfect to check out the list himself. Instead, he went straight to the classroom line like we're supposed to. But Old Fakey Fake was giving him the news when Joselyn and I finally made our way back there.

She was like (and now imagine that my voice is as frilly as a tutu), "Oh, Dylan, I'm sure you'll win. You'll be so good."

And he was all (and now imagine that my voice is low and perfect), "Thank you, but I haven't actually won yet." When he finished talking, he glanced down the line and caught my eye for a second. Then he looked away without saying anything.

Maybe I was imagining things, but I do think he looked at me with a twinge of respect, a kind of maybe-Susie-B.-will-prove-to-be-some-serious-competition respect. And I thought to myself . . . hmmmm . . . perhaps Mr. Springer told him about my essay and now he is actually worried about losing.

When I mentioned this to Joselyn, she jabbed her finger into my arm. "Susie B.," she said very seriously. "You are my best friend, but I have to say something here. Don't get cocky!" Then she explained that the only way we will even come close to winning is if we never forget about the winningness of Dylan and Matt.

And she is right, Susan B. Anthony! Don't be all, "You are being too modest for words, Susie B. You probably can be a little cocky because you wrote such a good essay!"

No! It's not true! I can't be even a tiny bit cocky because more bad news. According to the official list of candidates, Dylan Rodriguez is not my only competition. There are *three* people running for student council president. Three! Me, Dylan Rodriguez, and Soozee Gupta. That's right! Soozee! First, she stole my name and came up with a much more fascinating way to spell it, leaving me to be the one who uses an initial—even though I like the initial now—and now she is stealing my dream of being president of Mary Routt Elementary School!

Do you understand what this means? Do you understand how bad this is? Now not only will Dylan Rodriguez win just because he is perfect, but he will win because he is running against two girls with the same name, and if that is not confusing enough for people, I don't know what is! My own name, which I love so much, might be the very cause of my doom!

Oh, Susan. I wonder if you ever faced a pickle like this one. It would be like . . . remember that time you marched down to the polling station and told everybody that you were ready to cast your ballot?

They told you, "Are you crazy, lady? Women can't vote!"

And you said, "Um, yeah, the Fourteenth Amendment to the US Constitution says all citizens get the rights of citizens. I'm a citizen. Voting is a citizen's right. So—duh—I get to vote. Now, please get your ugly face out of the way because Imma do it!"

And then you got arrested and it was in the newspapers and everything.

Remember how you were so proud of that? Well,

now imagine that you did all of that and the news-papers said it was some other Susan who got arrested for voting and not you. Or worse, imagine that all that happened and neither of you Susans ended up in the newspaper. Instead, imagine that the papers said some man got arrested for doing what you did, and imagine that this man got to be in the paper all the time any-way, and that everyone thought he was so wonderful, and they even put his face on a cereal box. Maybe then, maybe if that had happened, you would know how I feel.

But hold on! Don't feel sorry for me. I am not inter-ested in your pity! I've just got to find a way to make sure everyone can tell the two Susans running for president apart, beat the most usual-genius boy in school, save the polar bears, and get everyone to sup-port freedom for paragraph writers.

I can do that, right? I mean . . . that sounds doable. Don't you think?

Dear Susan:

I know you have probably been worrying about me. I haven't written in my Hero Journal for a few days, and the last time, I was all, "Ack! Good news!" Then I was all, "Ack! Bad news!"

You were probably saying to yourself, "Poor Susie B.! She's up! She's down! She's the yo-yo of Southern California!"

But everything is all right. I have just been busy.

The day after my last letter, Principal Hodges invited the people running for office to a meeting. Now, even though it had the technical term "meeting," some of us candidates suspected that it might be a secret little celebration for us, a way of saying, "Good job on those essays, people!"

Still, I didn't have too high of hopes—not like Soozee, who thought there might be apple juice and cookies. Ha! That just shows why she wouldn't be a good president. She may be nice, but she doesn't understand this place at all! There was no way there would be cookies.

This place is practically the sugar police. They're worse than my mom! But I did think the principal might give us each a sugar-free peppermint, or maybe a little participation ribbon, or a little certificate that said "Good Job" or something.

But get this! It wasn't a celebration at all! It was a very serious "conversation."

It was in the multipurpose room, and we had to sit on hard folding chairs set up in a circle so that we could all see one another squirm around.

Principal Hodges was in a chair too. It's funny, but she sort of reminds me of you, Susan B. Anthony. She wears her hair in a tight bun, and her mouth curves into a natural frown. Even when she is happy or trying to balance on those tall shoes that she wears all the time now, she looks a little angry. She tries to cover it up by having a super-happy way of talking. But she can't smile all the time. We see the frown, and I think all of us suspect that—under the right conditions—she could be a mean one.

She looked at her watch. Then she looked up again and very friendly-friendly thanked us for wanting to serve our school.

She paused. For a long time, she paused. And she looked at us.

I thought, *Maybe she wants us to say something?* So, I raised my hand, all prepared to explain that I am ready to not just serve the school but to also basically save the world because that is the kind of president I am planning to be.

But I guess Principal Hodges did not see my hand because she started to talk again. Her voice got faster and faster, and a little less friendly-friendly, as she told us that we needed to remember that student council is a very serious business that means early mornings and helping with assemblies, wrapping-paper sales, jog-a-thons, and other activities that raise money for extras, like new balls for the playground.

But mostly, she said, being on student council means being a leader. She said if we're elected, younger students will look up to us. They'll be watching us even when we're not helping the school, like at lunch, when we're on the playground, and even when we're doing stuff around town. She said that how we act will affect how they act.

Suddenly, she didn't sound so nice anymore. She sounded like a mom, like a don't-try-any-monkey-business-with-me mom, like a this-natural-frown-on-my-face-is-because-I-can-see-right-through-you mom.

She said, "Are you ready to have all those eyeballs watching you? Are you ready to be a good role model?"

Then she really did look right through us! Her eyes met each of ours, and we knew she was seeing our brains, our veins, our blood, our thoughts. She was seeing all of us! This wasn't no game. This was *student council!*

She pointed toward the door and told us that if we were not ready for this "responsibility," we might as well leave and that no one would think less of us if we did.

Not one of us moved a muscle. But inside my head I was doing shuffles and buffaloes and all the best tap-dancing moves. I was thinking, *Leave? Now? Are you kidding me? You are only making me want to be president even more! People looking at me wherever I go? People saying, "There's Susie B. She is student council president of Mary Routt Elementary School"? That's eternal glory! Yes! Please!*

Of course, no one left. Even if they wanted to leave, they would have been too embarrassed. Principal Hodges may have said, "No one will think less of you," but everyone knew that people would think less of them, maybe not a lot, but at least a little.

Principal Hodges clapped her hands, and it was like a magic spell lifted because we all started to squirm a little uncomfortably. And then we started to squirm a *lot* uncomfortably because, suddenly, she got that famous look in her eyes, her favorite look, the look that means: it's time for *rules!*

Rule number one: understand the job you are running for! The president leads the student council meetings and says the Pledge of Allegiance at assemblies. The vice president takes over if the president is sick. The secretary writes notes on the meetings. The treasurer counts the money the student council helps raise. Everyone, no matter what elected position, helps at school events.

Rule number two: understand what your job isn't! No one in the student council can boss anyone around. Not teachers. Not teachers' aides. Not students. Not custodians. Not yard duties. Not lunch assistants. No to all bossing! No to all bossing always!

Rule number three: run a fair election!

No promising to do things that you know you can't do.

No giving people campaign buttons with pointy ends that could poke someone.

No giving people cupcakes or candy or sugar of any kind because our school does not want kids all hyped up on sugar when they are supposed to be learning.

No posting anything about us, our opponents, or our

school on social media because we need to protect one another's privacy and not encourage cyberbullying.

No bribing people for their votes, or threatening people for their votes, or having anyone else bribe or threaten people for their votes, because that would be cheating.

If we break any of these rules—bing, bang—we will be immediately kicked out of the campaign.

You're probably thinking, "Geez Louise! What the heck *can* you do?"

There were rules for that, too.

Rule number one: we can each hang two posters—only two. We can hang one near the lunch tables and one on the walls outside the classrooms. Posters must be printed on poster board. They must be twelve by eighteen inches. They must be posted vertically, not horizontally. They must be hung using painter's tape so that we don't ruin any paint or walls or anything at all.

Rule number two: we each have to give a five-minute speech at the big election assembly on the day before the election.

When Principal Hodges had tired us out with all the rules and made our mouths hang open from extreme rule-explanation boredom, she asked if we had any questions.

I just wanted to be clear on something, so I raised my hand. "If we are elected," I asked, "can we give important speeches about important topics that are very important?"

She shook her head and told us no, but that we *could* pass out programs at the winter concert.

Finally, it seemed like it was time to go back to our classes. Then—it was weird—Principal Hodges seemed really tired, and she never seems tired. Her shoulders were slumpy and the feet peeking out from her shoes were all pink. She said she wanted to give us a final warning.

And that sounded very intriguing, like movie-intriguing. So—even though I could barely stay still anymore—I leaned in and listened hard.

In a very gentle voice, she explained that she had seen a lot of these elections, and that that meant she had seen a lot of strange and unexpected things. What they were, she didn't say. But she wanted us to know that winning isn't everything, that it's your sportsmanship that matters. It's your sportsmanship that tells people the kind of person you are. She wanted us to think about that, and she wanted us to be good sports-people.

Everybody nodded, but if you looked closely at their

faces, you could tell they were thinking, *Sportsmanship, shmortsmanship. Winning is what matters. Winning is what makes you a winner.*

It made me feel a little nervous, to be honest. Because if winning makes you a winner, does losing make you a loser? That seemed very close to usual-genius kind of thinking, and you know how I feel about that. There are lots of things I don't win at. I don't win when I play chess with Joselyn. I don't win at getting solos at school concerts. And when I was on a soccer team before I started tap, I was the worst player on the whole team. I was always losing at soccer. Even if our team won, I still kind of lost because one time I even made a goal for the other team.

But I don't think I'm a loser, and I don't want other people to think I'm a loser either. And I don't want to think *other* people are losers. I want to think we are all just as good as Dylan Rodriguez! Because we are!

Still, I really do want to win.

We were excused back to class.

I looked at Dylan. He was staring down at the ground, and I could tell he was thinking hard about how much he wanted to be president. He was thinking so hard about it that his eyes were almost watering. He would not be easy to beat.

Then I looked over at Soozee. She was chatting away with Principal Hodges, who was walking us back. All bubbly and happy, Soozee was saying how fun it would be to get to help with school events, and then she asked if she could help at school events even if she didn't win.

That was some smart thinking, I thought. Getting the principal on your side was never a bad idea. I looked at Soozee more closely. Cool-spelled name. Cool hats and scarves. Cool French braids. She would be serious competition even if Dylan weren't running. Plus, she has twin sisters in third grade. So, you know, there goes the youth vote.

Dear Susan:

Here is a little pickle for you. It is something I didn't think of when we were having our meeting with Principal Hodges. But now I can't stop spinning about it.

If student council members don't have any bossing responsibilities and aren't allowed to give important speeches on important topics, then how can I do anything to support all the rights of all the people and polar bears, and also free the paragraph writers?

Dear Susan:

Here is another pickle. If we can't really do anything as student council members—if we can only go to meetings and help out with things like winter concerts—then are we being suckered into helping for free? Is there a bit of a switcheroo going on? That's what I'm asking.

Dear Susan:

The question is: If it's a switcheroo, then this whole student council business is kind of a scam, isn't it? Think of it this way. An apple is a fruit. A donut is delicious. Those are just basic facts that everyone must accept because they are true. Right? Well, this is a basic fact too: a president gives speeches and bosses people around. If I am president, I should get to do those things. If a president is not allowed to do those things, are they really a president?

Dear Susan:

If student council is a scam . . . do I want to be on student council?

Hmmm. There is still the big microphone action. You know that I do love that.

And there is the glory of people admiring you, which I still think seems pretty good.

And there is the fairness. Anyone would be better than Dylan.

And aren't those the reasons I was running in the first place?

But still . . . scams.

But still . . . big microphone action.

Dang!

Oh, big microphone, what is this power you have over me?

Dear Susan B. Anthony:

Hello.

Good day to you. One interesting thing about you is that you have your face on a dollar coin. Interestingly, I happen to receive such a coin every time one of my baby teeth falls out, which doesn't mean I believe in the tooth fairy. It just means I'm in it for the cash. That is all I have to say about that.

Dear Susan B. Anthony:

Hello.

Good day to you. One interesting thing about you is that you lived near the famous African American abolitionist Frederick Douglass. You were good friends with him since he was really smart and you both wanted to abolish slavery. But maybe the definition of "good friends" was different in your day—or at least it was to you!

Dear Susan B. Anthony:

Hello.

Good day to you.

Perhaps you have noticed the unfriendly tone of my last two letters. The truth is, I am very angry with you.

Why? Three words: George Francis Train.

Ha! You didn't think I'd find out about him, did you?

Well, I did! Two days ago, our class went to the media lab. We were told to use the internet to research a time our hero had to make a difficult choice. Oh, and you had a doozy!

It was after the Civil War. People wanted to give Black men the vote. There were lots of reasons for that, including—duh—fairness, but also because lots of people believed that if Black men couldn't vote, they wouldn't be able to protect themselves and their families from evil racist laws and stuff.

You and your gal Elizabeth were like, "Hey, America! If you are going to give Black men the vote, why not give it to women—white and Black—at the same time?

That is a genius move!" And you tried to get all your old abolitionist friends to agree with you.

But your pals were like, "Listen, that is a great idea, but it will be hard enough to give Black men the vote. The country will have to pass a whole constitutional amendment about it—the Fifteenth Amendment—and that is going to be super hard. If we add ladies, the amendment will fail for sure, because, you know, sexist yuckball-ism."

"But women should get to elect people too!" you said.

And they were all, "I hear you, but how about we do it one at a time? First, we work to give Black men the vote. Then we work to give women the vote."

But you were all, "No way! That stinks! Votes for women! Votes for women! I'm outta here!"

And you *were* out of there! You and Elizabeth Cady Stanton broke away from all your friends in the one main suffrage group, and you formed your own group.

Now, Susan B. Anthony, I really think you did the wrong thing there. It seems like you were being a big baby. Yes! You felt cheated and mad! I would have felt that way too! But extending the vote for some people—especially people hurt by evil racist laws—was better than extending the vote for no people.

Still, if this was all you had done, I would have

thought, *Well, Susan B. Anthony fought against slavery before she even fought for women. She really truly did believe in racial equality. I am going to let that one issue of not supporting the Fifteenth Amendment slide.*

But that was not all you did, was it? You basically told people that you would cut off your own arm before you would—and I quote—"ever work or demand the ballot for Blacks and not women."

You said that! I wrote it down straight from the internet. I checked multiple sites to make sure that it wasn't fake, and it wasn't fake. It was real. (Actually, though, you didn't say "Blacks." You said something that Lock told me isn't a nice word anymore. NOT the *really* bad one, but still a bad one.)

You know what I think, Susan B. Anthony? I think it sounds really racist. It sounds like you were saying that it would be a cold day in *h-e*-double-hockey-sticks before you would want Black men to vote and not white women.

Was that what you meant? Was it?

Ha! Don't lie to me! Because—remember—George Francis Train!

I looked him up! He was this really rich, racist white guy. You joined forces with him even though he loved slavery! You went on a whole campaign trip with him, and everywhere you went, he said bad things about Black people, and your whole life afterward you told everybody that George Francis Train was the greatest thing since sliced bread.

You threw Frederick Douglass under the bus, Susan B. Anthony, and not just that. You broke his heart.

You broke a lot of your friends' hearts.

You broke my heart.

Oh, I can practically hear you whining, "Oh, Susie B. It wasn't like that. I was just super upset that people wanted me to give up my life's work and campaign for Black voting rights before women's voting rights."

Liar!

Because it wasn't just George Francis Train, was it?

Many years later, when Black suffragists came to you and asked for your support, you were all, "Oh, sorry, dudettes. You know I'm with you, but I can't publicly say so because then I'll annoy all the racist white ladies who support suffrage . . . and I can't annoy them. So, yeah, bye."

Buh-bump. Did you hear that? That was the Black women you threw under the bus next to Frederick Douglass.

You know what? I bet you were never even friends with Madam C. J. Walker.

If she had said to you, "Um, I actually do have a yacht and I would love you to come on a trip with me," I bet you would have answered, "Oh . . . so sorry . . . uh . . . I wish I could . . . but, um, I can't be seen with you. . . . It's nothing personal. . . . Bye!"

Geez, Susan B. Anthony. Did you ever really believe in liberty and justice for *all*? Or did you only believe in them when it helped you, when it went along with what you really wanted?

PS: Did I ever happen to mention that Lock is Black? That's right! My mom had him when she was married to her first husband, Dan, who is African American. So, one, I would hate you for doing what you did no matter what. But, two, now you are messing with my family. So you are not just dead—you are dead to me.

Oh! By the way, Mr. Springer's favorite T-shirt reads, CHECK YOUR BIAS AT THE DOOR. I'm sure he will agree with me when I say that I need to find another hero for my Hero Project. Goodbye forever, you two-faced biddy!

Dear Susan B. Anthony:

Guess how Mr. Springer looked when I told him how you threw Black people under the bus? He looked like I was stabbing him in the heart!

He said he never would have guessed you weren't perfect.

Bad news for me, though. He also said we were too deep into the Hero Project to change topics. That means I'm stuck with you.

Here is a question for you. You know how you believed the Quaker idea that everyone is equal because we all have a God-given Inner Light? If that's what you really thought, how could you campaign with George Francis Train?

Dear Susan B. Anthony:

These are some words that George Francis Train said when he was campaigning with you: "Woman first, and negro last, is my programme."

That's the guy you chose over Frederick Douglass. *That* guy!

Dear Susan B. Anthony:

Today I am REQUIRED to tell you something that has been keeping me busy lately. Not that it is any of your business, Miss Snake Lady, but I have been working on my campaign posters. As you know, we can have two of them.

Fine. I will tell you more—but only because I need to get this off my chest, not because I want you to know.

Friday, after tap class, Joselyn and I went to buy poster supplies.

Now, I don't know what happened before Mom and Lock picked us up, but they seemed mad at each other. It was probably about Lock's transfer plans because Mom is always bugging Lock about his university applications, and Lock is always telling her to mind her own business.

Anyway, when they're mad at each other, they share their mad with everyone. Mom was trying hard to hide it because Joselyn was there. But Lock was giving us all the silent treatment. But not the complete silent treatment, just the I'll-bark-orders-at-you-but-say-nothing-else silent treatment.

As soon as we got to the store, Lock—who knows I love glitter—said we needed to stay away from the glitter aisle because glittery campaign posters would look "girlish."

I could not put up with that! That was a word bomb against girls *and* glitter. And let me just say this about that: no one should have to live a glitter-deprived life! But before I could tell Lock off, Joselyn—who is normally as much of a glitterati as I am—began agreeing with him. She said it will already be hard getting boys to vote for us since Matt Chan is very friendly-friendly with the sports boys and Dylan Rodriguez is the most popular kid at school.

Whoa, I thought, *I've been magically transported to Oppositeland*. It was like the Lock and Joselyn saying these things were the Oppositeland versions of the *real* Lock and Joselyn. Hating on glitter? Hating on girls? And now this business about popularity?

I tried to set the record straight. "Popularity is a middle school thing. We don't have to worry about that."

But that didn't set the record straight! Joselyn looked at me like *I* was the one from Oppositeland!

I stopped right there in the aisle—because I did not like seeing those Oppositeland eyeballs staring at my face. I told her all about how Lock had said elementary school was different and that, in elementary school, no one even thought about popularity. By this time, Lock had walked over to the Starbucks inside the store, so he couldn't back me up, and I don't think my mom wanted to back me up because she just kept pushing her cart and moving along.

Joselyn sighed, and she almost looked like she was a little embarrassed for me. She said in a very convincing voice that maybe things were different in Lock's day, but—now—popularity is a fifth-grade thing. A big fifth-grade thing. She said, and I quote, "Everyone in fifth grade knows that."

She wasn't mean about it, but it kind of felt like she was saying I should have known that. That made me wonder: Why didn't I know that? Then I remembered how my parents had tried to tell me this same thing, and how, actually, now that I thought about it, even Lock hadn't sounded too convinced when he said popularity started in middle school. I mean, he hadn't been in Lockdown mode at all. He'd been more like in . . . *meh* mode.

I admit it. I think they might be right, Susan B.

Anthony. I think popularity actually is a fifth-grade thing! And I guess that means we do have to worry about it, because guess what? According to Joselyn, popularity is like money! They both make people want to do things for you—even vote for you.

We got to the glitter aisle. I peeked in.

Next to me, Joselyn pushed back her hair, swinging the colorful little dolls that dangled from her earrings back and forth.

She wrapped her pinkie finger around mine and whispered, "I just want to do this campaign right. If we *can* win, I really want to win. You know, you've got Lock, but I've got Melissa, and Melissa is as annoying a usual genius as anyone."

That was true enough. Just last year Melissa had won the middle school science fair *and* been chosen for her AYSO division's All-Star team, which only the best soccer players in the whole town get to be on. Both of those things happened about the same time that Joselyn and I were cast as dancing chickens seven and eight for Dylan Rodriguez's Martha Washington solo.

I knew it was hard for Joselyn to admit that her own sister was a usual genius. It's bad enough going to school and knowing that the teachers think a bunch of other kids are smarter than you. But to go home and know your family thinks that too? That would be hard.

I didn't give that glitter one more thought. If the people are anti-glitter, we will not use glitter. If you need boring posters to beat usual geniuses, popular people, athletes, and helpful girls, then boring it is.

But I still say glitter is the salt of the decorating world. It gives everything oomph.

Dear Susan B. Anthony:

More election planning to report.

You're never going to believe this, but you know how Dylan is the most popular boy in my school? Well, guess who the most popular girl is?

And stop it, Susan B. Anthony! No, it's not me! Even I know that! Don't think buttering me up will make me forget about the terrible things you did.

It's Old Fakey Fake herself! It's true!

I didn't believe it when Joselyn spilled those beans when we were back at my house making our posters. But it does explain why people seem pretty eager to compliment her hair and clothes, and why they all wanted to go to her birthday party a while back. Even the sports girls wanted to go—and they're the first people to roll their eyes at any sign of nonsense.

Personally, I don't understand it at all. She's so mean!

But Joselyn says the right kind of mean can make you popular. She saw a whole musical about it last summer.

Of course, Chloe is never going to vote for me or Joselyn. She's for sure going to vote for Dylan and probably Matt. And if Chloe isn't going to vote for us, then none of her people will vote for us, which gets us right back to square one. Even the most boring posters in the world won't make Chloe change her mind—not when she's loved Dylan since probably forever.

But aha! My best spark has it all figured out! We don't need the Chloe vote—not when, with just a little bit of luck and speechifying about improving the prizes for the jog-a-thon, we might be able to get the I'll-do-anything-for-a-Frisbee vote! That's right! Do you know what people got for participating in last year's jog-a-thon? Bandannas that read, BULAGOO TIRES COME IN FIRST. But kids don't want no stinking bandannas that sell tires. They want fun stuff, like video games and iPads. Of course, there is no way this cheap place is going to offer up prizes like that. So Frisbees it is! Oh, yes. Frisbees will pave our paths to victory. I can feel it in my bones. Hurrah!

Dear Susan B. Anthony:

I don't even know why I am still writing to you since you are definitely not my hero, but I do admit that I like the way you never talk back. I especially like that you are not talking back today, because I am *not* in a listening mood.

I bet if you could talk back, you would probably say, "Gee, that doesn't sound like you, Susie B. I know that I am dead to you because I've been passing myself off as a hero when, in fact, I'm just a lady who let racism get in the way of protecting people's Inner Lights. But you not wanting me to talk back? Hmmm . . . that doesn't seem right."

How dare you say that, Susan B. Anthony? You don't know anything about me!

Today was a great day! An amazing day!

Today was the day we got to hang our campaign posters. Joselyn's mom took us to school early to hang them.

Joselyn's poster was very serious and impressive, with big, dark green letters that spelled out, "Joselyn $alazar for Trea$urer!"

Did you notice how she made the two Ss look like dollar signs? Yeah. Joselyn is brilliant like that. She is always good at mixing stuff up and making you see things in a different way. Her posters are like: money is straight up in my name, so of course you will want me for all your money-counting needs.

I was going to put, "Susie Babuszkiewicz! All the Rights of All the People and Polar Bears All the Time! Free the Paragraph Writers!" on my posters, but there wasn't room. So Joselyn recommended, "Susie Babusz-kiewicz! She's Presidential!"

Now, here is the great thing about that slogan: it says, "Hey! That Susie B. is presidential! It doesn't matter that she's not popular. She's a real leader who will be a role model on the playground AND when she uses the big microphone. Wow! I want to vote for her!"

Besides that, I put a big color photo of my face right on my poster—and now, when everyone hears my speech, they will put two and two together and say, "Oh, Susie B. is the sandy-haired winner we have been waiting for. We want her—not the girl with French braids who spells her name in a very fascinating way. And definitely not Dylan Rodriguez, whose popularity is nothing to Susie B.'s presidentialness!"

Speaking of Dylan, am I a little worried that his posters say "DONUTS" in giant red letters?

Ha! Not at all.

Well, possibly a little. I mean, it's not just me, right? That slogan is a real grabber. Don't you think? And, if we're being honest, it's more than a grabber, right? It's more like a choke hold. It's more like a slogan that squeezes your throat and shakes you a million ways until all you can think is: *Wait! Point me toward these so-called donuts!*

But am I worried that Dylan's idea to run on a donut platform is genius because who can say no to donuts, especially if the candidate offering the donuts is already on a commercial for Bitty Donut Nature Crunch cereal?

No. I am not worried about that at all.

Joselyn did some sneaky-pants sneaking, and so we have valuable information. Here is what happened: In class we were making campaign posters for our heroes since Mr. Springer seems to think that learning is connected to our lives or something. He says since the school is having student council elections, our class should also have hero elections. There will be posters, and we will all give short speeches about why our heroes are so great, and—as a class—vote for the best hero of all time.

I was very busy convincing Carson that he couldn't make a cubist campaign poster that was all blues and grays—even for Picasso, who I guess really loved blue and gray. I told Carson that adding glitter to a campaign poster was one thing, but making a poster that was just a picture was another.

But Carson was being very stubborn. He insisted on making his poster as arty as all get-out. Without making any goofy sounds or winking or doing any of the things that usually make people grind their teeth and go, "Stop it, Carson," he simply said, "For once, I actually get to do art with you guys. I'm not gonna waste it."

While I was talking to Carson about that, Joselyn was on the other side of the room being all *La, la, la. I'm just coloring away on my poster for self-made millionaire Madam C. J. Walker.* In fact, she was listening to these two boys talking about Dylan.

Casually, in this oh-I-don't-really-care-about-this-topic-but-if-you're-going-to-talk-about-it-then-just-talk-about-it way, she asked them, "What's the deal with Dylan writing 'donuts' on both his posters?"

One of the boys told her all about it. He explained that Dylan's plan is for the student council to sell donuts every Friday morning and then use the money to have a big, end-of-the-school-year, blowout party that includes a bounce house, a waterslide, and other cool activities.

But ha, ha! Remember? Candidates are not allowed to make promises that they cannot keep! That is one of the *rules*! And there is no way the school will let them have a giant party that is as wild as a waterslide birthday party! This school is opposed to danger and fun and sugar, and so, of course, they are extra opposed to actual sugar-sponsored dangerous fun! They won't even let the kinders and firsties climb to the top of the big climbing dome! For sure, they won't let Dylan bring in a bunch of wild waterslides! Waterslides are basically head-lump machines!

Oh, yes, people might first think, *Yum. Delicious Donuts Equal Wonderful Waterslides!* But very quickly they will use their minds and know that it will never happen.

Then, when they see my posters, they will be reminded that I am *presidential*—which is what you want in a president. Plus, they'll also hear my speech and learn that I will try to get the school to give out *Frisbees* as jog-a-thon prizes! And I will help at school events, and lead people in the Pledge of Allegiance, and just be a wonderful role model who happens to support all the rights of all the people, as well as the suffering polar bears and paragraph writers.

And all of the voters will wisely say, "Susie B. makes such good sense! I'm voting for her and not this lying donut promiser."

And they will not vote for Soozee Gupta because her slogan is "Work Hard, Play Hard," and when I told Lock that, he said, "No one has used that phrase since 2005, so get with the times, other Susan."

So—yeah—I am feeling good about the election! Really good.

Dear NOT Susan B. Anthony:

That is what I am calling you now: NOT Susan B. Anthony. You are NOT Susan B. Anthony because, while I have a lot of things I need to say—and I need someone to say them to—I do not want to say them to a person who went around blowing out Inner Lights. So, I am saying them to NOT you.

Anyway, NOT Susan B. Anthony, I need to tell you that I am not feeling good about the election. At lunchtime, Dylan brought donuts for the entire fifth-grade class. He just dished them out like he had permission. And you know he *did not* have permission! You know we were specifically told not to tempt people with sugar!

At least they were not fresh donuts. They were the little powdered sugar Hostess kind. But that's how he got away with it! He had them hidden in the most gigantic lunch box you have ever seen, and he sneakily went around giving one donut to every kid, saying, "Remember, a vote for Dylan is a vote for donuts—and waterslides."

And he was so sly that the lunch assistants didn't see a thing.

I was running to the front office, ready to turn him in, when Joselyn yanked me by the arm, saying, "You can't be a snitch, Susie B. Then you'll never win!"

Of course, she was right. I looked around, saw all those happy, powdered-sugar-covered faces smiling up at Dylan. I realized that I could never be the person who denied people Hostess donuts.

And then a worse thought came to me: *What if people don't care about a person being presidential?* What if all people really want are donuts and waterslides that they will never see? How can anything I do compete with the memory of a soft donut caking your hand in fluffy white sugar?

Dear NOT Susan B. Anthony:

What if I snuck everyone Oreos? The Oreo is the king of store-bought cookies. Oreos totally beat out Hostess donuts. Right?

Dear NOT Susan B. Anthony:

Oh my gosh! Matt Chan totally stole my Oreos idea! He squeezed white frosting cent signs on Oreo cookies and gave them to everyone. What a Dylan Rodriguez!

Dear NOT Susan B. Anthony:

Well, the shoe is on the other foot this time! When Dylan Rodriguez gave everybody donuts, Joselyn was all, "It's not that big of a deal. People don't even like donuts," even though—let's face it—EVERYONE loves donuts.

But now that Matt gave everyone Oreos, Joselyn is going ballistic.

"He's buying their votes!" she said as Old Fakey Fake waved one of Matt's delicious Oreos right in front of her face and then walked away, smiling.

I shook my head. Of course he was buying their votes! He was a handful of Oreos away from buying *my* vote! Obviously, we were doomed.

But I didn't even know how doomed we were! By the end of lunch every fifth grader was running around with Oreo smears on their teeth, and all the fifth-grade boys—and a few of the girls—were now wearing Matt Chan stickers on their chests and bracelets strung with Bitty Donut Nature Crunch on their wrists.

Frisbees, I told Joselyn, could never compete with this.

Joselyn looked out on the playground. Her eyebrows got all crinkly, like they do when she is playing a tough chess match. I could tell that the wheels in her head were turning. Oh, they were turning something good.

"It is on," she said in a dangerous voice. "It is so on."

My palms began to sweat. As much as I had thought about giving out Oreos, I had never really meant it. I didn't want to do anything that would get us in trouble, which made me wonder suddenly: Why would Dylan do something that could get *him* in trouble? For all I knew, Matt was a big cheater frog. Maybe bribing people with Oreos is his style, but Dylan is normally so perfect . . . too perfect. So why cheat? I rested my fist under my chin, feeling very Sherlock Holmes, as I shared these ideas with Joselyn.

"Don't you get it?" she asked. "Perfect people are the *most* likely to cheat."

I didn't understand what she meant.

She explained that, apparently, perfect people will do anything to keep all the winning to themselves. Like, if she wins treasurer, she knows Melissa will turn around and decide, "Oh, I guess I've just got to be ruler of the whole world now." And then Melissa will stop at nothing until she is.

From the handball courts came a loud sound. It was Old Fakey Fake, and she was not even being fakey-fake. She was being real—real mad! She was yelling straight in the face of Dylan Rodriguez.

She was all, "Fine! I don't want one of your stupid bracelets after all. I wouldn't want one if you *did* have enough for everyone. I wouldn't want one if you paid me a million dollars. I hope you lose that stupid election!"

Then she stomped off with Rachelle, Rachel, Rose, and four other girls trailing behind her, and— shocker!—she almost walked right into Matt.

But Matt's face wore the worst possible expression that he could have worn: glee! He had seen everything— the whole scene between Dylan and Chloe, the whole way Dylan must have said Chloe couldn't have a bracelet, and the whole way she got mad about it. Matt had seen it. And he thought it was funny. More especially, he thought the way Dylan dissed her was funny.

And Fakey Fake saw the glee! Oh, she really saw it, even though right away he tried to hide it behind an open hand.

Fakey Fake's body went stiff. She huffed, "I hope you lose too, Matt!"

Joselyn's head slowly turned toward mine, and it

was like a spark had lit inside her. She looked back at Fakey Fake, and then she looked back at me, a big grin spreading across her face.

I took a step back, finally figuring out what she was thinking. "No," I said. "Uh-uh. Never. No way."

She said it was the only way. She said, "The better-jog-a-thon-prizes plan is out the window. You can see that. We need to grab our chances where we find them."

But I told her that I was not making nicey-nice to Old Fakey Fake, that I'd rather lose, that I have principles.

And she said that if we didn't get on Chloe's good side while we could, we *would* lose.

"Who would you rather Chloe support?" Joselyn added. "Soozee Gupta? Soozee Gupta's twin sisters are named Persimmon and Pomegranate. We can't compete with that!"

I pulled the roots of my hair. Buddy up to Chloe? It would feel so yucky! It would feel so cheaty. But . . .

Joselyn said one last thing. She said it super light, super milky-frothy. "Hey, hate the game, not the player."

I didn't even know what that meant.

Joselyn put her hand on my shoulder and laid it all out for me—slowly, so I could write it in my journal. She said we didn't make the game. We didn't decide that school elections were about popularity. We were just pawns, like in chess. We only had the little bit of power that we had. We could either use that power or get knocked off the board.

I bit on the end of my pen, letting one more big, stinky truth about our messed-up world sink in. On the surface, it seemed like all of us candidates had the same chances. We got two posters. We got one speech. But there were all these hidden moves that people had—and some of them were straight-out cheating, like the Oreos and donuts, and some of them were not cheating, like the teachers all loving Dylan and wanting him to win, and Matt being almost famous for being a great athlete. What chance did a couple of pawns like me and Joselyn have against those things? If Dylan and Matt were using hidden moves, then why shouldn't we? And what other hidden move did we have but sucking up to Chloe? It was the only thing that would keep us from getting knocked off the board.

Joselyn lowered her voice and told me that Melissa had been chosen as student of the month at the middle school. The notice had come home the day before.

Well, rotten eggs and people who don't recycle! How could I say no to her plan after she added that?! Now it wasn't just about trying to balance the scales of fairness—it was about being a good friend to Joselyn. I didn't come out and say I'd do it, and I didn't say I wouldn't do it. But I knew. In my heart I already knew. I was going to fakey-fake Old Fakey Fake.

Dear NOT Susan B. Anthony:

An unexpected twist! Fakey-faking is harder than it looks. Watching Chloe, you would think it would be easy. You would think you would just have to brush the knots out of your hair, wear the nice dress you refused to wear on Thanksgiving to school, and tell Chloe that her campaign poster for some lady named Helena Rubinstein was amazing and that it was the best thing you'd ever seen with your perfect-vision eyeballs that have seen a lot, including the Grand Canyon.

True enough, those are the places you start. At least that is where I started the day after Chloe yelled at Dylan and set Operation Out-Fakey-Fake-Old-Fakey-Fake in motion.

We had a little slice of time between language arts and math, so Mr. Springer told us to finish up our posters since we'd start presenting them to the class the next day. I slid next to Chloe and pretended I was searching for a black crayon in Mr. Springer's bucket of extra crayons. Then I did a very convincing double take at her poster, like I couldn't help but notice the beauty before me and instantly compliment it.

But it turns out that you can't out-fakey-fake an expert. As soon as I started talking to her, Chloe squinted at me. Then, in a pleasant voice that did not match her squint, she said, "Ummm, sorry, but I'm not gonna vote for you."

I mumbled that I had just been trying to say something nice and rushed back to my desk. Luckily, Carson was so focused on making his cubist campaign poster for Pablo Picasso that he didn't notice how red my face had turned.

But Joselyn noticed! She was staring right at me all the way from her side of the room, and the disappointment on her face proved that she'd seen the whole thing, which made me even more embarrassed.

Guess what she did! She took a deep breath and pushed back her shoulders. Then she marched right over to Old Fakey Fake and said the last words I ever expected to come out of her beautiful mouth. Sounding annoyed, she said, "Is your hero really Helena Rubinstein?"

Here is why that surprised me: Joselyn may be the big brains of our friendship, but I'm the comeback queen. If Chloe throws a word bomb at me, I'm gonna throw out a comeback, and I'm gonna feel good about that comeback. It might not keep the word bomb from messing with me, but at least—I hope—it will keep Chloe from ever knowing. But Joselyn has a totally different way of dealing with things. Her attitude about word bombs is that you should avoid getting them.

If you don't want a word bomb from Chloe, then stay out of Chloe's way. That's what Joselyn says.

But, I think, how is that even possible?! Chloe is right there in our class! No one can avoid her.

And now here Joselyn was, right in Chloe's face, acting like Chloe had insulted her or something. It didn't make any sense. We were supposed to be nice-ing Chloe into voting for us, not making her mad at us.

Chloe didn't even look up at Joselyn. She just said she wasn't voting for *her*, either.

Straightaway, Joselyn made this little *tsss* sound and added, "Don't flatter yourself."

Joselyn's voice had been light, but not so light that Chloe's ears didn't turn pink.

"Ooooooh," whispered Carson, which made me wonder if maybe Carson had heard my short conversation with Chloe.

But I couldn't think about that then. I had to focus on the now. I was thinking, *What the heck are you up to,*

Joselyn, you master chess player? What kind of crazy move is this?

But Joselyn didn't even look at me, so I didn't know. She didn't give any clue that this had anything to do with me, or the election, or our big fakey-fake plan. Instead, with more of a normal, not-annoyed voice, she said that she just wanted to know if Chloe had really chosen to do her Hero Project on Helena Rubinstein.

And Chloe, in her special I'm-perfect-because-I'm-popular way, said, "Duh. Of course! Helena Rubinstein is my hero, and she is awesome because she basically invented the beauty business, and all I care about is looks and stuff because I'm so popular and pretty and never have messy hair and everyone thinks I'm great."

Okay. She didn't say exactly that, but you get the picture.

But—aha!—Joselyn revealed that Chloe was a big old liar! Helena Rubinstein did not invent the beauty business. Joselyn's hero, Madam C. J. Walker, did. Most people just don't know that because Madam C. J. Walker was Black, so her story was practically erased from history.

Chloe, of course, could not put up with Joselyn calling her a liar. She went on about how Helena Rubinstein had had this really hard life, and that she had

had to move from Poland to Australia just to get out of marrying some gross guy her parents were trying to pawn off on her, and that when she got to Australia, she didn't have any money. Plus, she barely spoke any English, and people were mean to her because she was Jewish.

But Joselyn was like, "You think that was hard? Madam C. J. Walker was born right after the Civil War. Her parents were slaves."

And Chloe was all, "Well, Helena Rubinstein went on to become one of the richest women in the world."

Joselyn said that didn't matter because Madam C. J. Walker was still the first self-made female millionaire in the whole United States of America.

But Chloe had moves in her yet. She pointed her finger right at Joselyn and asked *when* Madam C. J. Walker became a millionaire.

When Joselyn said it was in the 1910s, Chloe's face squeezed right up, and I could tell she was really thinking about things. Finally, she admitted that she didn't remember when Helena Rubinstein became a millionaire, but she thought that maybe it was later than that.

Then—and you are not going to believe this—Chloe actually admitted that it was way cool that the first woman in America to make a million bucks was Black.

When Chloe said that, I couldn't help it. I fell back in my chair and yelled, "Wow!" I mean, how had Joselyn done that? How had she started sounding annoyed at Chloe and ended up getting Chloe to admit she had a really awesome hero?

But again, I couldn't worry about those things at that moment because, suddenly, everybody was looking at me—including Chloe and Joselyn.

So I just grabbed Carson's Pablo Picasso poster right out of his hands and held it up in front of everyone. Sure, I told the class, Carson's poster didn't look very election-y, but it did look very cubist. "In fact," I said, or sort of said—it was something like this—"this incredible work of art looks like the most cubist picture in this room. It probably deserves to be hung on the wall, don't you think, Mr. Springer?"

Of course, Mr. Springer just told me to get back to my work, and he didn't even offer to hang Carson's picture of Picasso where Dylan's cubist portrait of Steve Jobs still hung.

Usual geniuses!

Dear NOT Susan B. Anthony:

I have been talking to Joselyn, and I have more information about our Fakey Fake plan.

Joselyn was at the ice cream store last night because—durgh, of course—her family had to celebrate that Melissa made first chair violin in the middle school orchestra.

Anyway, who do you think walked in but Chloe and her mom?

Aha! thought Joselyn. *This is the perfect time to work on our plan!* So she asked Chloe if she wanted to get a table together.

Surprisingly, Chloe agreed.

They sat together and had a conversation, and it turns out that they both chose their heroes not because they had anything to do with the beauty business, but because they were rich businesswomen, and Joselyn and Chloe want to be rich businesswomen one day too.

And now they know they have something in common.

Boom!

Do you know what that means, NOT Susan B. Anthony?

It means Joselyn and I are gold! Because—apparently—the whole key to a successful fake-out is to find a common interest with the person you need something from. First, you find something you have in common. Then, you get all friendly. And finally, they vote for you!

Joselyn explained everything at lunch. We were sitting on a bench watching Chloe and the three Rs play basketball, but we were also being very sly, so they didn't realize we were watching them. And as we were watching, we were also talking, and Joselyn was telling me that to out-fakey-fake an old fakey fake, you don't actually fakey-fake at all. You just be yourself, except you try harder to connect with the person, and you agree with them whenever you can and sometimes also when you don't if it's a little thing that doesn't matter, and plus you forget all the ways they've been mean to you.

Now I just have to find some things that I have in common with Chloe too, and then—abracadabra—it's big microphone time for me and counting dollars time for my best spark.

Dear NOT Susan B. Anthony:

Mom was running even later than usual today. She got me to school just in the nick, so I was running to my line when something made a smile burst onto my face.

Joselyn, Chloe, and a bunch of girls were laughing *together*, like they were the best of friends.

Joselyn looked over and caught my eye. Then she said something to Chloe and bolted toward me. She held up this book. It was called *The Big Book of Badass Businesswomen*. Her mom had just bought it for her. It had information on Madam C. J. Walker and also Helena Rubinstein. Joselyn thought Chloe would like it—and she did.

"It's all happening," Joselyn said, giving me a quick hug. "Soon, all those girls will be Team Us, and—unexpected benefit—we will be Team Them. Won't it be great when we not only win, but also have so many new friends?"

Well, I didn't know about that. I wanted the Chloe

vote, but I sure didn't think we needed new friends—especially of the Fakey Fake variety. But there was no time to get into that. We needed to celebrate the success of Joselyn's brilliant plan. And what better way to celebrate than through the beautiful art of dance?

Mr. Springer came, and the class started to follow him to class, but that didn't stop me. I started to pump my elbows and shuffle-step forward. Joselyn squeezed my arm. She pointed her chin at Chloe, ahead of us. I looked just in time to see Chloe give Dylan an angry look and then start spit-whispering to her friends.

Woo-hoo! She was as mad at him as ever! Maybe we really would be elected! I kicked my heels and gave Joselyn a happy thumbs-up.

Dear REAL Susan B. Anthony:

Sadly, happiness is like a bug. It's always getting squashed.

When we got into class, it was time for our poster presentations.

This was not what squashed my mood. I was excited for my presentation. I couldn't wait to tell everyone NOT to vote for you for best hero of all time. That's right, Susan B. Anthony! Psych on your face! I was ready to spill the beans about how you only supported racial equality when it was convenient.

Mr. Springer asked us who wanted to go first.

I shot my hand in the air.

But, of course, who else do you think raised his hand?

That's right! Dylan Donut-Head Rodriguez.

And Mr. Springer was all, "Oh-ho! It's our two presidential candidates." He said "to be fair," he would flip a coin to see who got to go first. Naturally, the coin chose Dylan.

Dylan stood up. He pulled out his poster about Steve Jobs.

Okay, I can admit this. Dylan's poster was good. It was not a brilliant work of art like Carson's, but it was fine. It had this big drawing of a happy-looking Steve Jobs. He wore a black turtleneck and had a golden halo over his head. The headline at the top of the poster read, "Steve Jobs, Visionary."

Dylan went on and on. Oh, Steve Jobs was one of the founders of Apple. Oh, Steve Jobs changed the way we think about computers and phones and design.

I was thinking, *This Steve Jobs guy sounds like a real usual-genius type. Who wants to hear about him?*

All of a sudden, Dylan stopped. He grabbed his poster and tore it in half! In half, I'm telling you! He threw the pieces on the ground, and when he was sure every person in that room was staring at him, he pulled out another poster. This one also had a picture of Steve Jobs. He was still wearing a black turtleneck, but in this drawing his face was purple and mean, and it had little red devil horns. The headline read, "Steve Jobs: What a Jerk!"

A little ping went off in my head, and I thought, *Uh-oh. I have a bad feeling about this.*

Dylan went on to tell us about all the people Steve

Jobs treated like garbage. He bullied them, yelled at them, made them feel bad about themselves. He had this one daughter. He barely even blinked at her for, like, ten years. It didn't seem to matter to him at all that she and her mom were hardly scraping by in the world, and this was when he was one of the richest people alive.

Dylan said that when he started his project, he thought Steve Jobs was one of the greatest people of all time. Now he would say Steve Jobs was amazing and creative and important, but he wouldn't call him a hero. Dylan wouldn't even call him a good human being.

When everyone was finally dizzy from learning what a deadbeat Steve Jobs was, Dylan told us one last thing. He said, "Vote for anyone you want for best hero of all time. But don't vote for Steve Jobs. He doesn't deserve it."

For a moment, the class became completely quiet. Not a sniffle, not a butt squirm, not a chair squeak. Then—boom—everyone went wild. They started whistling, cheering, pounding on their desks.

Mr. Springer patted Dylan on the back and said he'd never seen a "braver" presentation. "I'm so impressed," he told us all. "I'm just so impressed!"

Dylan walked back to his desk. He fell in his chair

like he couldn't stand it anymore, like his disappointment in Steve Jobs was this heavy boulder weighing him down.

I didn't know what to say. Dylan Rodriguez had stolen my presentation! Well, not technically. But he'd definitely taken my thunder.

When everyone was finally recovered from the miracle of Saint Dylan-of-Inspiringville, Mr. Springer motioned at me. It was my turn to give my presentation.

I gave it. What else could I do? But I could tell by everyone's embarrassed glances at their desks that they thought I was copying Dylan. They thought I hadn't put a presentation together at all. But I had! Of course I had! And it was good! So then—because I'm me—I had to get mad at those embarrassed glances.

I told the class, "Don't think I just copied Dylan. My hero was as much of a jerk as Steve Jobs. Don't vote for her, either."

I pointed at where it said "Susan B. Anthony—two-faced biddy" on my poster.

"See?" I said. "Why would I write that there if I weren't going to tell you not to vote for her?"

Everybody just looked at me like, *Oh, no, Susie B. You're losing it.*

Mr. Springer rubbed his jaw. "You seem a little angry,"

he told me, and then, acting like he was doing me a favor, he told me to get some water from the outdoor water fountain and come back to class.

I saw what was going on. When Dylan Rodriguez puts devil horns on Steve Jobs, he is brave and inspiring. When I call you, Susan B. Anthony, a two-faced biddy—I'm angry.

I should not have said anything. I can see that now. But if there is one thing my butterfly brain is not good at, it's shutting the heck up. My big fat mouth blurted, "Girls can be angry, Mr. Springer. It is their right!"

He nodded calmly. "Yes, Susie B. But not during class time."

I walked back to my desk, ignoring Mr. Springer's suggestion that I go get myself some water. I didn't need water. I needed people to see my work, to call me brave and inspiring. But that wasn't going to happen. That never happens.

When I walked by her desk, Chloe whispered, "That's not very 'presidential.'"

Around her, everyone giggled.

"You're just mean!" The words erupted out of my mouth. That's right. They erupted. Like lava from a volcano. Because I was a volcano. A volcano of 😣, and everyone could see it.

"Please, sit," Mr. Springer said, even more calmly than before.

Chloe turned her head one way, then the other. "What?" she said innocently. "I didn't do anything."

Mr. Springer clapped his hands and called for the next volunteer.

As soon as I took my seat, Carson leaned in and gobbled sympathetically.

When I snorted in reply, he whispered, "I think you should be able to get mad."

Well, that did it. My eyes just welled right up, and all that anger inside me melted into hurt.

I looked down at my desk, and when I looked up again, Joselyn was shaking her head at me, disappointed. I knew what she was thinking. All her good fakey-faking. I'd flushed it down the toilet.

And I still don't think anybody appreciated what a nonhero you were, Susan B. Anthony. In the end, all they saw was me acting mad. They didn't see you at all. My mom was right. Nobody likes angry girls.

Dear NOT Susan B. Anthony:

This was my lunch:

1. Lunch bell rings.
2. As usual, I walk straight over to Joselyn so we can go to the lunch tables.
3. Joselyn races ahead of me.
4. I say, "Joselyn, wait up."
5. She says nothing.
6. I sit down at the table where we normally eat.
7. She goes straight to Chloe's table and says, "Can I join you guys?"
8. "Sure," says Chloe. "Boy, that Susie B. sure has anger-control problems."

It was horrible. Do you know what happens when your best spark ditches you, NOT Susan B. Anthony? You're sparkless! You're just . . . cold meat loaf and mashed potatoes and everything else that is nasty and gross until you heat it up.

Carson saw the whole thing. At least I think he did. Why else would he have sat down and offered to eat with me?

Of course, when he did, everyone at Chloe's table burst out laughing.

Without meaning to, I glanced over at them. The three Rs were craning their necks in my direction. Joselyn looked down at her sandwich, the tiniest smile on her mouth.

I turned back and offered Carson a peanut-butter-filled pretzel.

I wish I could say that I looked confident and enthusiastic, but I think I probably looked like a sad, soggy french fry that no one ever wants to eat because it's just limp and pale and gross and friendless.

Carson didn't seem to take it personally. He just ate the pretzel and then went to town on his mac and cheese.

It was kind of interesting to watch him. His fork moved so fast that I'm not sure he ever had a chance to chew.

But you know what? It kind of perked me up to watch him. That was some straight-up talent he had there. I told Carson he should enter one of those food-eating contests. He could win big money.

He gave me a thumbs-up that was like, *Thanks for noticing, Susie B.!*

He took his apple and said he could eat that super-fast too, except—when he tried—he swallowed too big a piece. His face turned purple, and he started coughing all over the place. Finally, he just had to spit everything out and drink some water.

I told him, "Listen, Carson. Don't be like that guy in the Greek mythology books. He made wings out of wax and flew too close to the sun, but the wax melted and he fell in the ocean. Just because you have a special talent doesn't mean you should think you're not going to choke on a giant piece of apple." Or, well, I said something like that. It definitely involved the Greek dude, who I just read about last night.

Bottom line: I liked having lunch with Carson, especially the part where he didn't choke to death. He's nice and funny and so good at art *and* eating fast. But here is the thing. He's also not the best friend I've had forever who suddenly won't even talk to me and is sitting with Old Fakey Fake, laughing and giggling like the happiest person in the world. One Carson does not equal one Joselyn. That is some seriously heavy math there. And you know what they say about math. It is what it is.

Dear NOT Susan B. Anthony:

Surprising development! Joselyn called me. Well, she called my mom since I don't have a phone, but she wanted to talk to me.

At first, I was like, "What? Calling to stab me in the back again?"

She acted like she didn't know what I was talking about.

I reminded her about lunch, and she let out this long sigh.

I needed to have more faith in her, she said.

It was all part of the plan, she told me.

"Trust me," she said. "You really blew it by calling Chloe mean."

I said I was sorry, and I really meant it. I had ruined all her good fakey-faking.

But apparently, that wasn't even the half of what I'd ruined. Get this. This whole time I've been thinking Chloe was mean, she and her friends have been think-ing *I'm* mean!

I know! I couldn't believe it either. It made me so mad. How could anyone think I'm mean? I support all the rights of all the people, polar bears, and paragraph writers. That is literally the opposite of mean!

But Joselyn says all my good comebacks hurt their feelings. They told her that at lunch.

Of course, I reminded Joselyn that I only give good comebacks in self-defense. But she says Chloe and them don't see it that way. They don't believe they ever say anything that deserves a comeback. They think they are nice.

Hold on to your bonnet, Susan B. Anthony. When I snorted at the ridiculousness of that, Joselyn said, "Actually, they are not that bad. I kind of like them."

My knees started to buckle. I had been standing in the kitchen, and I had to grab on to the refrigerator so I could slide down to the floor without clunking my head against the hardwood.

What was going on? Chloe and her friends were not that bad? Joselyn kind of liked them? We were back in Oppositeland!

Joselyn started to speak, her words picking up speed as she did, like she just had to get them out before I could stop her. But I couldn't stop her. I didn't have a single blurt in me—and when has that ever happened?

She said something like, "They're nicer than we thought. Do you know that their Girl Scout troop feeds the homeless once a month? Or that they volunteer every Sunday at a bunny rescue? And, now don't get mad, Susie B., but you talk a lot about saving polar bears, but do you ever *do* anything about polar bears? Or anything? They are out there saving bunnies every week."

All I could do was mumble strange sounds. It was possible I was dying from my brain exploding.

We don't have to out-fakey-fake them at all, she explained. We just have to be friendly. Because they are friendly. "That's better anyway, right? It's more honest."

I tried to get a hold of myself, but things still weren't making sense. I grabbed at words like they were doors to normalcy. Better? Honest? What?

"But, see, you've got to let me repair your reputation. You've got to hang tight while they get over you calling Chloe mean. Then I can convince them you're not so bad."

"I'm not so bad?"

"Exactly! Don't talk to me at school. I'll take care of it. Just give me a few days. We can still win this election! You still want to win, right?"

Winning! How could I think about winning? All I

knew was that the world was upside down. Opposite-land had got a hold on me and would not let go.

There was so much to stew on after Joselyn hung up. How had they fooled her? What mischief-y business had they been up to? How could I un-mischief it? And what was this stuff about me "hanging tight"? Everyone knows that I don't hang tight. I bulldoze right along. That is part of my charm.

I just—ack!—I'm so confused . . . and angry . . . and bulldoze-y. I think . . . me turning Hulk! Me want smashy-smashy! Me want breaky-breaky!

Dear NOT Susan B. Anthony:

Oh my gosh. Well, let me tell you. Going all Hulk is not the answer.

Obviously, I had to talk this whole Chloe/Joselyn/hang-tight situation over with my brother. So when I was finally able to peel myself off the floor, I marched over to Lock's room.

He was sitting at his desk, squeezing his head and staring at his laptop screen.

I not-very-nicely Hulked that I needed advice.

He flung himself back in his seat and said, couldn't I see that he was studying.

So I Hulked a little more Hulkily that it looked like he was watching YouTube.

And he Hulked even more Hulkily that he was allowed to take breaks.

And I Hulked very Hulkily that, whatever he was doing, he didn't need to yell at me.

And he shouted, "I am not yelling at you, but I can't stop everything I'm doing every time you have some little problem. I have my own life to worry about."

Well, that hurt! I took a step back.

"Fine," I said, Hulking more Hulkily than the queen of Hulkiness. "Be that way! But I just wanted your opinion on a very important issue that affects my whole life and dreams!" I didn't even wait for him to answer. I just bulldozed right ahead. I stomped my foot and told him about my phone call with Joselyn. I said I couldn't just "hang tight" while people fooled her into believing they were nice—not even for the election, that that would be against my principles.

At this point, Lock was supposed to take a deep breath, calm himself down, and say, "I apologize! I didn't realize you were dealing with something *that* important! I'm here for you, you sweet little sis."

But that is not what Lock said. That is not even close to what Lock said.

He snorted—at me! "Your principles," he laughed. "Don't worry. Everyone knows all about your principles, Suze. You make sure of that enough."

I took a step back, confused. It sounded like he was insulting me, but—if that were the case—it didn't even make sense. I said, "Of course I make sure everyone knows about my principles. You told me to!"

A look like he had just eaten something nasty crossed his face.

"You did!" I shouted, pointing at him. "You did and

Mom did! You both told me that I should always stand up for what is right. So, I do."

His shoulders fell forward as his tongue kind of rolled around outside his mouth. "Ugh. There is a difference between standing up for what is right and being a pain in the butt."

I took another step back. A pain in the butt? Me? What was happening? I was back in Oppositeland.

He spread out his hands, and his desk chair began to swivel. "No matter what it's about, you always have to be right. You always have to have things your way. Of course, people are going to think you're mean if you act like that and if you can never let a single thing go. You know what your problem is, Suze? You're high-maintenance. You are the most high-maintenance person I know."

Or, well, he may not have said exactly that. But only because I boiled it down to the basics.

Question: Did you ever feel like you were living in a cave seeing only shadows, and then—click—suddenly someone turned on the light and showed you that your whole life was a lie?

I'm telling you right now, it's the worst! Basically, I always thought I was a lovable warrior for justice who helped everyone by standing by my beliefs and telling the truth. And now here Lock was calling me a pig-headed, high-maintenance pain in the cushy tushy.

It was like the light turned on and the shadows fell away. I remembered Joselyn: "They think *you're* mean." I remembered Dad: "No one likes all the getting mad." And Mom: "People don't vote for angry women." And Mr. Springer: "You seem a little angry." I remembered every time anyone had humphed and rolled their eyes at me because they didn't want to hear one more word about all the rights, all the people, all the polar bears, all the anything—or maybe that wasn't it. Maybe that had never been it. Maybe they just didn't want to hear one more word . . . from me.

I stumbled, a dizzying hum filling my head. Could it be true? Did I not know myself at all? Was I high-maintenance? Was I annoying? Was I mean?

I ran out of Lock's room and made my way, some-how, to Mom and Dad. They were snacking on cheese and crackers while cooking dinner. They looked like they didn't have a care in the world, which I suppose they didn't because how could their problems compete with mine?

I threw myself into a kitchen chair. All wobbly and insecure, I asked, "Am I high-maintenance? Am I annoying? Am I mean?"

Their eyes got big, and they gave each other *a look*. It was a look that said it all. It was a look that said that I—Susie Babuszkiewicz—am a big ol' pain in the you-know-what! Even my parents, who are supposed to adore me without any second thoughts or complaints, think so! And no one likes a big ol' pain in the you-know-what.

Seeing this truth about myself? Well, it was bright, and it was ugly. I raced to my room, where I fell on my bed and cried! That's right, I cried. And I never cry! I didn't even cry when I learned that there are only, like, five thousand black rhinos left in the world, or when I found out that there are millions of girls who don't get to go to school just because they are girls.

Usually, I am almost famous for being the kind of person who falls and gets right back up again. That is what my parents always say is so great about me. That is what helped me to become such a good reader—and tap dancer, too! I did not start out a great tap dancer. It took me way longer to move up to intermediate tap than all the other kids who started when I did. But I did not give up! I kept at it! I took home the Most Determined award two years in a row! And it's because I am chock-full of grit! But I was not full of grit this time. For all I knew, my grit had hitchhiked to Florida or places unknown.

Mom knocked on my door. "Can I come in? Do you want to talk? I don't think you're high-maintenance. I don't think you're annoying."

But I knew she was lying. I yelled, "Go away!"

Then Dad knocked on the door. "You okay, Suze? Want some cheese and crackers?"

But how could I choke down crackers when all my spit had transformed into tears? I yelled, "Leave me alone."

And then Lock came, and when he said it was him, I shouted, "You're right! I'm high-maintenance!"

Lock opened the door and didn't even care when I said, "You're invading my space! You're invading my space!"

He plopped down on the foot of my bed, squeezed my foot. Very soothingly, he told me to get a grip, that I was better than this.

I threw my pillow over my head and said that it wasn't true. I wasn't better than this. I was a gigantic pain in the cushy tushy who people think is mean, and when they see me, they gag and go, "Ergh! Not her again!" And even my best friend thinks I'm "not so bad," which implies at least a little bad. And pretty soon she probably won't even want to be my best friend anymore because why would anyone want to be best friends with someone who makes their butt go, "Holy moly, that hurts!"

Lock tried to make me feel better. He was like, "Walk back from the cliff, Suze. Walk back from the cliff." Then he apologized for upsetting me and said he was just in a bad mood because he was having a hard time in biology. "I don't really think you're high-maintenance," he said. "And anyone who calls you mean doesn't know the meaning of that word."

I gave him a look like, *Yeah, that's some pretty fancy tap dancing. And I would know!*

"No," he told me. "It's true. Are you determined? Yes. Do you feel things strongly? Yes. But those are good things."

I rolled over in my bed. He lied some more about how great I am. Then, finally, he left.

Soon, it was time for dinner. I went downstairs, ate. Everybody acted like, *Oh, everything is back to normal. Let's all pretend that that unpleasantness never happened.*

So I pretended too. Because—you know—I didn't want to be *high-maintenance* or anything. I didn't want to be all *Susie Babuszkiewicz.*

But here is the problem, NOT Susan B. Anthony. If I am not going to be all *Susie Babuszkiewicz*, then who the heck am I going to be?

Dear REAL Susan B. Anthony:

I know.

It's been a few days.

I've been trying to be all low-maintenance, and low-maintenance people are too chill to be writing down their opinions and thoughts all the time. No one wants to hear all that yak, yak, yak—not even the dead people they are writing to.

Low-maintenance people are just sort of, "Whatever, dude." Like when their best sparks ignore them in the name of repairing their reputations, low-maintenance people shrug and think, *Whatever, dude. I'm chill.* And when their friend Carson says, "Hey, do you want to go to other Soozee's Emergency Preparedness Club and practice escaping from avalanches," low-maintenance people are all, "Whatever, dude. If that's what you want." And when tattletales like Chloe say loudly in class, "Uh, Mr. Springer, Carson is drawing and whispering 'avalanche' when we're supposed to be reading," low-maintenance people just bite their tongues and clench their teeth and start singing "The Star-Spangled Banner" in their heads while trying to keep their big mouths shut.

So . . . anyway . . . whatever, dude . . . I thought I should at least tell you that you and Steve Jobs weren't the only disappointments in the hero department.

Yesterday, the last kid finally gave her hero presentation, and, honestly, every one of those heroes turned out to be worse than the first. It was like me and Dylan opened the door to criticizing famous role models. Carson said Pablo Picasso was crazy sexist, and Fakey Fake told us that Helena Rubinstein could be a big phony. ~~And she would know!~~ (Sorry. That wasn't low-maintenance.)

Back to the presentations: Have you ever heard of President Franklin Roosevelt? He did a lot of good things for workers, retired folks, and poor people during some really hard times in American history. Plus, he had a woman in his cabinet (and he was the first president to do that). You know that I approve of that message! But during World War II, he forced Japanese Americans to stay in concentration camps. Isn't that awful?

Even George Washington and Thomas Jefferson turned out to be duds. They both owned slaves even though they fought a revolution for freedom. At least

George Washington freed his slaves when he died. Thomas Jefferson? He had hundreds of slaves, but when he kicked the bucket, he only freed the ones that were his own children—although he wouldn't even admit that they *were* his!

And—you'll never believe this one—Martin Luther King Jr. cheated on some big paper he had to write to get his PhD. In some parts, he just said word for word what some other guy had already written.

Obviously, some of those things were way worse than others. If I were to rank the horrible horribleness of these particularly not-perfect people, I would definitely say that George Washington, Thomas Jefferson, and Franklin Roosevelt were worse than you. But I would also say that the horrible horribleness you did was way worse than the horrible horribleness of Helena Rubinstein or Martin Luther King Jr.

My dad thinks I am learning a very important lesson, which is that all people are affected by the times they live in. You can't expect them to live outside their own "historical bubble." But I think lots of your friends tried to live outside their historical bubble. Like you, they were surrounded by the idea that white people were better than Black people, but they fought against it.

"Yes," you're probably saying, "but you're thinking

of my buddy Frederick Douglass, who had once been a slave. Of course *he* thought that."

Oh my gosh! You are the worst, Susan B. Anthony! Accept some responsibility for your actions already! I was actually thinking of women like—

"Sure, like Sojourner Truth," I hear you rudely interrupting. "But she was Black too."

Just stop talking, Susan B. Anthony! Now you're just digging your own grave!

Yes, I am thinking of Sojourner Truth—owner of the best name in the history of all names ever. She'd been a slave like Frederick Douglass, and she went to all the Women's Rights Conventions, and she called out racism and sexism wherever she saw them.

But I'm also thinking of Lucy Stone.

Ha! You didn't think I knew about her, did you? You're not the only important lady in all the books about important ladies, you know! Lucy Stone is in all of them too! She was white, and she never threw Frederick Douglass under the bus!

Obviously, I chose the wrong women's rights pioneer to make my hero. But it looks like I'm stuck with you awhile longer. Apparently, this Hero Project is going to continue until the end of time—or at least until after Mr. Springer's latest big assignment.

Get this, it's a Hero Parade. We're going to decorate shoeboxes so that they "tell a story" about our heroes. And then we're going to prop the shoeboxes on little wheels so we can pull them around the blacktop. The fourth graders get to come watch and everything. That is what makes me think that maybe this dang hero stuff is almost over. Nothing in school says, "Goodbye! See you never!" more than showing off for younger students. It's not until next week—a few days before the election. But don't worry, Susan B. Anthony. I will be sure to write and tell you what the fourth graders think about your racism. Ha! That's right! I'm not sugarcoating the truth just 'cause those kids are little. They have the right to know that you weren't so great! You made big mistakes, mean mistakes, and those mistakes need to be seen as much as your fighting on needs to be seen. I will tell everyone. . . .

WAIT!

STOP!

Let me take a deep breath and find my low-maintenance chill.

Okay. I'm better.

I'm better-ish.

Oh, brother. Who are we kidding? I'm not better-ish. I can't even stay low-maintenance while writing letters to a dead lady. How useless is that?

It's not like you can change now, Susan B. Anthony. It's not like any of those heroes can change. So why bother complaining about them? Why bother holding on to principles when it doesn't even matter? When it just drives away your best spark and makes your family think you're a pain?

And yet here I am. Being a total Susie Babuszkiewicz, even when I started out trying not to be.

Maybe people are just who they are.

Maybe they can't change. I mean, you kept putting white women's rights over Black people's lives.

Maybe I can't change either. Maybe I'll always be a blurty, high-maintenance bigmouth.

But I don't want to be a blurty, high-maintenance bigmouth.

☹

Dear REAL Susan B. Anthony:

I've been thinking about it, and I'm not going to be like you. I'm not going to keep making the same mistake over and over again, even when I should know better.

I *will* be a better Susie B. I will be a Susie B. who makes everyone say, "There's Susie B. She sure is low-maintenance. Let's give her eternal glory!"

The problem is, I'm not really sure what low-maintenance looks like . . . besides being chill. But how chill is chill? Is it chill to have *some* principles? I'm not supposed to have *no* principles, right? I mean, that sounds wrong. I've got to have at least a few principles. But where is the line between too little and too much? Where is the line between low-maintenance and high-maintenance? How will I know when I find it?

Dear REAL Susan B. Anthony:

Today we are supposed to write our heroes and tell them "how we feel" about the hero election results.

~~The good news is you lost, so ha, ha for you.~~

The news is that Helena Rubinstein won.

You're thinking, *What the heck-y? She beat Martin Luther King Jr.? He obviously should have won because of civil rights and only a little bit of cheating in school.*

Why you gotta be that way, Susan B. Anthony? Helena Rubinstein was an important businessperson. She showed the world that women could lead big companies. You must like that! Also, she gave millions of dollars to charities. You should be happy for Helena!

"Fine," I hear you saying. "Hooray for Helena Rubinstein. But you at least voted for Martin Luther King Jr., right?"

Okay. It's complicated.

I'm going to tell you what happened, but this story starts with some embarrassing information. Please be a mature person about it.

Last night my dad got home from a short business

trip. He promised that he would make me one of his famous smoothies for breakfast and even take me to school. But I think he put something weird in that smoothie. Around midmorning, I started to feel these little pings and pangs in my gut. After a while, those little pings and pangs turned into big bings and bangs. Then, suddenly, an emergency situation was about to erupt.

I ran to Mr. Springer and whispered, "I know you like us to use the bathroom during recess, but I gotta go now, Mr. Springer. Like, ten-minutes-ago now!"

The panic in my eyes showed him that I was not fooling around, so he nodded in a way that said, "Move quickly! And may the flapping wings of angels speed you along!"

Boy, did I run!

Well, I was wrapping things up on the you-know-what when all of a sudden I heard the bathroom door swing open. Quietly, a person slid into the stall next to mine and pushed a note under the divider.

I thought, *What's going on here? I'm not picking that up! This tile floor is gross.*

But then Joselyn whispered, "Pick up the note."

I did. It said, "If you are Susie B., tell me my middle name and how I got it."

"Eme," I said, "It's your grandma's name, the one

from Guatemala, the one who gave you the earrings you always wear."

"Correct!" she said, explaining that she'd needed to make sure it was me because she had a *confidential secret* to share.

Well, I do like confidential secrets, especially from Joselyn, who I knew had been working so hard these last few days to repair my reputation and probably had something important to say about that. But let's face it—this was weird timing. I asked her if we could discuss things a bit later.

Her voice firm, she said, "Shush. I only have a minute." Apparently, she'd faked a coughing fit just so she could leave the room. Mr. Springer had given her permission to get some water from the fountain, but if she didn't get back to class soon, she knew he would get suspicious.

"Listen," she said, using her best strategizing voice. "When it's time to vote for the greatest hero, you need to vote for Chloe's hero, Helena Rubinstein."

Then she explained that if I wanted to fix my reputation, I needed to bend, and this was one way to bend. Chloe really wanted Helena Rubinstein to win because every time she wins something, her mom takes her to Disneyland, and she really wants to go to Disneyland.

"You know the old saying," Joselyn said. "'You scratch my back and I'll scratch yours.' Do this for her, and she'll do something for you . . . like let you prove you're not mean."

My immediate thought was *no way*! I'm voting for MLK. Duh! He's way more important than Chloe's hero.

But then I thought of the whole high-maintenance thing. Here was a chance for me to practice low-maintenancing, to just be easy peasy and go with the flow. Shouldn't I? It would solve so many problems. Joselyn wouldn't have to repair my reputation anymore. I wouldn't have to hang tight anymore. Me and my best spark could be friends in public again. And—who knew—maybe I'd even earn the Chloe vote, and I'd win the election and get to speak into the big microphone, and be a role model, and . . . somehow . . . do some darn good in this world—at least as much good as people helping in a bunny rescue.

All the time I was thinking that, my principles were yelling, "Don't low-maintenance this! Your vote is your voice! You have to vote for the person you think should win!"

Well, Joselyn has known me a long time, and she must have realized that my principles were getting all up in my face.

Impatiently, she said, "Just do it, Susie B. It's the only way."

Without another word, she ran from the bathroom, sending the heavy door slamming behind her.

It was a doozy, Susan B. Anthony. It was a doozy of a hard choice. But as the day wore on, I slyly questioned my classmates about which hero they were voting for. Pretty quickly, it became clear that no matter who I voted for, the winner would be either Chloe or Dylan. That's right! People were going to vote for Steve Jobs not because they thought Steve Jobs was the best hero of all the class heroes, but because they thought Dylan was the most perfectly wonderful person ever born!

That was when my mind exploded. I suddenly understood that this hero election was its own kind of popularity contest. Since Dylan and Chloe were the most popular people in class, one of them was going to win no matter what. It was another one of those hidden moves of the game, the ones that made something unfair, even when it seemed fair. One vote. One hero. How much fairer could it get? But people weren't voting for the hero. They were voting for the kid behind the hero. Even if I had wanted you to win, Susan B. Anthony, you never would have stood a chance!

Bottom line, it came down to this: I could vote for Dylan, who absolutely did not deserve one more victory in his entire life. I could vote for Chloe, who . . . yuck. Or I could vote for Martin Luther King Jr., who I knew deserved to win. But that would basically mean throwing my vote away. And, instead of throwing my vote away, wouldn't it be better to . . . just close the closet door on my principles and make things easy for everyone, including me?

One time, my grandpa took me fishing. (Just follow along, Susan B. Anthony. This is going to make sense.) We caught these fish and put them in a cooler. When we got back to his house, they were pretty smelly.

Grandpa said something like, "If you're gonna fish, you gotta make peace with the stink."

Obviously, I never went fishing again. I was not going to put up with that nonsense. But maybe that's what you need to do if you want to be low-maintenance. Maybe you've got to . . . hold your nose.

Then again . . . you worked with that stinky fish George Francis Train, and his stink is still hanging over you.

Anyway, you guessed it.

I voted for Helena Rubinstein.

And now she has been declared the greatest hero of all time, at least according to Mr. Springer's fifth-grade class. And—get this—she won by one vote. She won by *my* vote.

And how does that stink feel?

It does not feel good. It feels stinky.

But do I think I made the right decision?

All I know is this. Guess where I'm eating lunch tomorrow? Chloe's table.

Dear NOT Susan B. Anthony:

Here is what people talk about at Chloe's lunch table:

1. How great Chloe is.
2. Hair.
3. TV shows.
4. Electronic games.

Now, I am not saying there is anything wrong with talking about these things.

~~Okay. Yes. I am saying there is something wrong with talking about how great Chloe is. And I won't do it! I will not do it! I don't care what kind of maintenance that makes me.~~

I have already mentioned that I greatly admire Soozee's French braids. But personally, I feel a tightness in my chest and a monkeylike need to jump around if I have to spend more than six seconds running a brush through my hair.

My butterfly brain says, "Help me! This is the most boring thing ever!"

As for TV shows and electronic games, well, that's just hard for me. I get one hour of non-writing-or-schoolwork-related screen time on school days and two hours on weekends. That's it. Plus, if it's not on Netflix or YouTube, I've never seen it. And if it's something having to do with an e-game? Give it up! My parents say gaming systems squash creativity. So I never know what anybody is ever talking about when it comes to that kind of stuff.

You would think it would be even harder for Joselyn. After all, she gets even less screen time than I do. But when Chloe and the three Rs start laughing about games, actors, or shows, Joselyn just nods and laughs along. She pretends like she understands it all, when I'm sure she doesn't.

I wonder if Chloe and the three Rs are sure about that too. Twice at the lunch table I saw Chloe get this sneaky glint in her eye as she asked Joselyn who her favorite characters were in the shows they were talking about.

Joselyn being Joselyn, she was pretty quick on her feet with an answer, but Chloe, Rachelle, Rachel, and Rose were just as quick at flashing one another a look that said, *Joselyn is clueless.*

Those girls tried their glints on me, too. But I didn't see what the big deal was about admitting you'd never watched something.

I straight up said, "I don't have a favorite character, and I don't know any of those shows. My parents are all about limiting my fun."

That interested them.

Rachelle threw her hair back and said, "Oh, that's so unfair!"

And Rose looked almost heartbroken for me when I told her I didn't have my own phone. She said there was no way she could live like that.

At the time this was happening, it seemed fine. I actually thought they were being pretty friendly, and I could tell Joselyn was happy we were all getting along. But—ha!—in the middle of the night I woke up wondering how nice they meant to be. Did they really feel for how hard it is to never get to text a friend? To not even know who some actress plastered on everyone's backpack and T-shirt is? Because didn't Chloe and her friends have the tiniest little grins on their faces when they were listening to me? And didn't they keep trying to hide those little grins every time I looked them in the eye? And if that was the case, didn't that mean that Chloe and her people were doing the old

switcheroo of planting confusion and doubt in seem-
ingly nice words? And shouldn't I speak up for myself
when this happens? But if I do that, am I being high-
maintenance?! I need to know!

Dear NOT Susan B. Anthony:

I talked to Joselyn about my switcheroo worries. It was before school started, when everyone was still getting in line. I kept it very low-maintenance. I didn't make it a big deal. I just said in a very soft whisper that no one else could hear, "Is it possible that by eating with Chloe, we are making it easier for her to be mean to us, and shouldn't we maybe not put up with that?"

She looked at me like I didn't make any sense at all.

I said, "Can't we go back to eating by ourselves now? I think my reputation has been repaired enough."

But Joselyn just kind of smiled. "It's more fun to eat with Chloe. When we're all together, I mean."

I thought my knees might buckle out from under me again, and this time I had no refrigerator to hold on to. How could it be more fun to eat with a bunch of people you barely know than just your best spark? But I held it together. I was as cool and quiet as the AC right after the guy comes to service it. I didn't creak or rattle once. And believe me, I felt like rattling!

Dylan came and lined up behind us.

Then, from across the playground, came Soozee. She was running, a pink-and-gold scarf wrapped around her neck, the ends flowing behind her. She stopped right in front of us. "Hold out your hand," she said.

Joselyn and I looked at each other, shrugged, and held out our hands.

She smiled at Dylan and told him to do it too.

Dylan looked very suspicious, but he did what she asked.

Into each of our palms she dropped a Shrinky Dink. They looked just like the I VOTED stickers grown-ups get when they vote, but they were smaller, kind of see-through, and hard.

In a total Soozee Gupta move, she'd made one for everyone running for student council. Just because she wanted to. Just because she was excited for all of us, and she wanted everyone to know that—win or lose— she was ready to help in any way.

Yeah.

That girl is weird, but good weird. And I loved my little Shrinky Dink. I yelled, "I love my little Shrinky Dink!" right there so Soozee knew it. For a minute I even forgot about what Joselyn had just said, and that is because I am actually a little obsessed with Shrinky

Dinks. But it is a funny obsession because I always forget Shrinky Dinks exist until I see some, and then I remember and say, "I want to make Shrinky Dinks too," but almost as soon as I say that, I forget and never make any. And then the circle starts all over again.

I was laughing about it with Soozee and Joselyn, and even Dylan was laughing, and it was kind of nice to see him laugh because—come to think of it—I hardly ever do.

Dylan even said, "This is really cool. Thanks, Soozee." He even put it in the little mesh pocket on the front of his backpack so everyone could see it.

In typical Soozee fashion, she was already thinking ahead. "Maybe we could make some more of these before the election! I have plenty of Shrinky Dink paper at my house. Or we could start a Shrinky Dinks Club!"

"Shrinky Dinks!" It was Chloe. She had gotten in line behind Dylan. Behind her stood the three Rs. She turned to them and said, "Remember in second grade? When they were so popular?"

For a moment, it was kind of like time stopped. And I could see that Soozee wasn't quite sure if she was being burned. She blinked, and her cheeks started to grow red.

Of course, I did think she was being burned. I thought

to myself, *This is a straight-up word-bomb situation.* Chloe was saying only little kids should like Shrinky Dinks, even though every living person should love them. And I was preparing my comeback when Joselyn suddenly squeezed my wrist.

She leaned in, whispered, "She didn't mean anything. They *were* popular in second grade."

"They are always popular," I muttered back.

"Just . . . Do you have to . . . ? Relax."

The air in my lungs went *pffffeeeewwwww*, like a balloon. And I bit down on my lip. Low-maintenance.

Soozee smiled and said she had to go to her line. And I do think her scarf had a little less perk in its flutter when she walked away.

"Hi, Dylan," said Chloe, ~~all marshmallow Peeps and little pink packets of sugar~~ all nicely.

"Ummm . . . I forgot to drop something off in the office," he said, sprinting away.

Rachelle, Rachel, Rose, and Joselyn huddled around Chloe as she asked them why he was being so mean to her. What had she ever done to him?

Maybe, I thought (because Joselyn would be very mad if I said it out loud), *Dylan Rodriguez has better taste than I give him credit for.*

Dear NOT Susan B. Anthony:

I was rocking a little bit of a zombie vibe when I walked into class. My mouth was open, and my eyes were blank-looking. I was probably green. It was because I think I might be allergic to being low-maintenance. Either that or I'm still not doing it right.

I just never know what to believe anymore.

What Chloe said to Soozee hadn't been a word bomb?

Really?

Carson took one look at me and said, "Gobble, gobble. You okay?"

One shoulder did a little lift and drop. "I'm chill."

At lunch I followed Joselyn over to Chloe's table.

Let me tell you this, NOT Susan B. Anthony. I was a delight! I was a delight of fun and charm! And I will admit that things started out okay.

For a breath of fresh air, Chloe brought up a totally different subject, one that I could join: music!

Chloe said how she liked this one boy band, and I

said, "Yeah, I am not opposed to that boy band." And then she brought up this one hip-hop artist, and I said, "Yeah, I am totally cool with that brilliant lady, and I especially like that she is not as skinny as a toothpick."

"Yeah," said Chloe, "but she would be prettier if she were thin."

Joselyn was sitting across from me. Her eyes bulged and she gave her head the tiniest shake.

I said nothing, even though my principles told me I should really say something.

"No!" I silently begged my principles. "No one wants to hear from you. Be quiet!"

"Agggh! We will not be quiet!" they growled in my head. "We want to be heard!"

Then Chloe said that if she doesn't grow up to a be a tech billionaire, she will probably become a professional hip-hop dancer.

I thought that was a fine thing to say, and I was happy to move the conversation along. I replied with something like, "Hey, that's cool. One day I'm going to be a professional singer/tap dancer."

That was when everything fell apart.

"Tap dancer? What kind of dancing is that?" asked Chloe, like she didn't even believe tap dancing was a thing, let alone a fantastic and wonderful art form.

"I know what it is," said Rachel, laughing. "It's really dorky." She stepped away from the table and did something that I guess was supposed to look like tap dancing, but she did it while mugging up her face and flapping her arms like a duck.

"Yeah," agreed Joselyn, laughing along with her. She turned to face Chloe. "Do you actually take hip-hop dance lessons, though? That would be cool."

You had to go back and read those last few sentences again, didn't you? You had to go back and see if you had been right the first time, if it had really been *Joselyn* who had agreed that tap dancing was dorky. And it was! Her words stabbed me right in the chest! Worse, she word-bombed tap dancing! And that *was* a word bomb! I knew it was. There was no maybe-or-maybe-not-ness about it. Rachel was saying tap dancing was dorky. Joselyn was saying tap dancing was dorky. And I will just say this about that: I have enough grit to survive this word bomb. But what did tap dancing ever do to Joselyn except let her feet become beautiful tippy-tappy musical instruments?

It was too much! But did I leave the table? Did I yell or scream or defend the greatest of all dances?

No. I sat there like a sucker, too stunned to speak.

And when Joselyn called me on Mom's cell phone

after school, I listened like a real sheep as she said, "That was fun today at lunch, huh? Wasn't that hysterical when Rachel did that dance? I almost spit out my milk!"

I tried to be low-key. Yes, it was hysterical, I answered. Yes, it had been funny. But hadn't it also been kind of insulting to tap dancing and to people who tap-dance? Like us?

She was practically moaning when she told me that it had just been a joke and then asked, "Why do you always have to take everything so seriously?"

"I've been trying not to," I said, feeling hurt that she hadn't even seemed to notice.

There was a pause, and Joselyn dropped the subject completely. Sounding all excited, she explained that— happy, happy—we've been invited to Chloe's Girl Scout meeting this Friday. It's right after school.

Of course, we have tap-dancing class then. When I reminded her of that, she was like, "Oh . . . right . . . well, I've been thinking of taking a break from those. It's not because of what Rachel said. I've been thinking about it for a while."

Well, I did not believe that. But I didn't say anything, and it wasn't because I was being low-maintenance. It was because my tongue was paralyzed.

So, instead of going to tap with me on Friday, Joselyn

is going to check out the Girl Scout meeting with Chloe and them.

And she's going to let me know how it goes.

And maybe, in the future, I can reschedule my dance class (even though we both know that Friday afternoon is the only time it is offered). And then I can try one of the Girl Scout meetings too.

You know. If I want.

Dear NOT Susan B. Anthony:

Similes that would make historical sense to my "hero" for National Simile Day

People are *like* figuring out how many days it would take you to get from Rochester, New York, to Portland, Oregon, on a train: complicated. Because apparently it would have taken you longer than four days, which is what I answered when we had that math assignment. I had guessed you could take one train from Destination A to Destination B, and that the train would never stop. But that wasn't the case. You would have had to take a bunch of different trains, and you would have had to stop and wait for some of the trains, and you would have traveled in more of a zigzag fashion than a straight line. In other words, it would have been complicated.

People are also *like* lions. Sometimes, an adorable baby wildebeest might see a lion at the everyday watering hole. The wildebeest might think, *That lion isn't so bad.* For a while, the lion might even act like the baby wildebeest's best friend and not try to eat it at all. But then, one day, when it least expects it, the baby wildebeest might turn around and find a bunch of lion teeth stabbing its neck. In the same way, sometimes a person might be sitting at a lunch table and really trying to think, *Oh, these people (including their best friend) aren't so bad*, but then that person will turn around and—boom—all of a sudden there's a bunch of lion teeth stabbing their neck.

But people are also *like* those buoy things you see bobbing in the ocean. When you're too tired to swim anymore, you can hang on to them. They will support you until you can swim some more.

My family has been very buoy-ish for me lately. When Joselyn's mom texted my mom that Joselyn was taking a break from tap dancing and wouldn't need a ride, my mom could tell something was wrong.

Dad was out of town, so she said we were going to have a special girls' night. We brought home a pizza. She let me choose a full-length movie for us to watch after dinner (even though it meant breaking our weekday screen rules), and she told me that as a special treat she was going to make us some popcorn.

I was still feeling pretty bad about . . . everything, but I figured I might as well work it. Pouting, I said, "Can we please, please, please have chocolate instead of popcorn?"

She put her arm around my shoulder and said, "Let

me see. . . ." Then she snuck off to her bedroom to look through her secret stash.

Lock found me on the couch scrolling through the Netflix menu. He sat next to me. He was dressed in his nice jeans, and I could smell his minty fresh breath, so I figured he must have been getting ready to go out with his friends.

I very pathetically whined, "Can't you stay and watch the movie?"

He swatted my arm. "No way. I'm outta here." He tapped his head against mine and whispered that Mom and Dad are worried about me. I guess they think maybe I'm having friendship problems, but they don't want to ask because they're afraid I'll bite their heads off. But since Lock wasn't afraid of me biting his head off, he said, "What's the deal?"

I sighed and explained that I was still having issues with Joselyn, but that because of all my low-maintenancing, I didn't know what to do. Saying nothing was making me miserable. But saying something would make me annoying.

Lock twisted his head to make sure Mom wasn't sneaking up on us. Then he pulled out a package of peanut M&M's and poured some into my hands.

I shoved them into my mouth so Mom would never

know. This was a rare double candy opportunity. I was not about to blow it.

He said that friendship stuff is always hard, but if you are having problems with a bestie, you have to talk to them about it.

Well, that was only a little confusing. I asked him what happened to him thinking I needed to be low-maintenance all the time.

He was like, "What? I never said that."

But of course he said that! I reminded him how he called me a big ol' high-maintenance pain in the cushy tushy, and then I explained that everyone else thought I was a big ol' high-maintenance pain in the cushy tushy too. "So, obviously," I said, "that means I have to be low-maintenance, even though being completely chill about everything is making me want to scream and yell and bite into things."

"Ugh," he groaned. "I told you I was sorry. I told you I was just having a bad day and that I didn't mean it."

But what did that matter? I knew everyone else meant it.

He pulled his phone from his pocket and offered it to me. "Just call Joselyn."

My principles were drumming inside me, saying, "Call! Call!"

Figuring I might as well shut them up, I took his phone and called Ms. Salazar.

"Oh, honey," she said to me, trying to hide her pity. "Joselyn isn't here right now. Should I have her call you back?"

I didn't need to ask where Joselyn was. Because where would she be on a Friday night? It's just her, Melissa, and her mom. If Joselyn wasn't with her mom, and she wasn't with me, obviously she was with Chloe. They had decided to do something together after that Girl Scout meeting.

Not even the little bowl of Hershey's Kisses that my mom gave me could help me recover from that one.

I was still thinking about it when Carson called and invited me to the Norton Simon Museum. He said he and his mom were going in the morning, and that if I still wanted to go, I could join them.

Well, that did pull me a bit out of my funk. The chance to see a real-life Picasso? Count me in!

"What about Joselyn?" he asked. "Do you think she'll want to come too?"

Blech. I was pretty sure I knew the answer. "I think she's busy."

So I guess I am taking this adventure without her, which leads me to my last simile for National Simile

Day: best friends are *like* mother birds. You can't always tell when they are about to abandon you in your nest and make you fend for yourself without even a little bit of regurgitated worm to eat. The difference is that when mother birds do that, it's because they are saying to their babies, "Hey, it's time for you to test your wings and be free." But when best friends do it, it is because they are the ones who want to be free, and they just want you to be eaten by some giant hawk who will come down and rip your head off.

Dear NOT Susan B. Anthony:

How is it possible that my family lives thirty minutes from the famous Norton Simon Museum, but they have never taken me there? All this time, I could have been seeing cool paintings by Picasso and a bunch of other dead artists that I would probably know all about if my parents had been more on the ball.

My favorite part of the day was when we sat down in this garden full of statues and had ice cream. It was Carson's favorite part too.

He said, "Art is always more interesting when there is ice cream involved," which I had to agree with, even though I was getting pretty wiggly since I'd also had a bowl of Hershey's Kisses and two big mouthfuls of M&M's the night before. And French toast for breakfast because I was still working my mom feeling sorry for me. And also some jelly beans in Carson's car. And a soda with lunch.

But you know what? I didn't actually mind feeling wiggly! I actually sometimes like it when my brain is flip-flapping around. Because here is a little secret. Just because I can have a hard time focusing on what other people are focusing on, it doesn't mean I can't focus on *anything*. And sometimes, the things I'm focusing on are way more interesting than the things everyone else is focusing on.

For example: paragraphs!

Ha, ha! You thought I was all done with paragraphs, didn't you? You thought, *Oh, man! The student council president can't boss anybody, so Susie B. sure as heck can't tell the teachers to chill out about paragraphs. I guess she'll never mention paragraphs again.*

Wrong! Win or lose, I may not be able to solve our school's paragraph crisis, but I still wanted to know why they were a *universal mystery*.

When we were strolling around the museum, I asked Principal Carson's Mom to spill the beans. Why were paragraphs a mystery? Why did we have to write paragraphs with as many sentences as grades we had? Lock was in community college. He didn't have a numbered grade, so how many sentences did he have to include in his paragraphs? And why exactly would anyone be afraid of paragraphs? They were way less scary than all the polar bears dying.

Carson was very curious about those things too. He

nodded right along as I hopped up and down asking my questions. And here is something interesting about that. You know how, at school, Carson is always winking and gobbling and stuff? Well, he wasn't like that at the museum. My theory is that Carson does those things because he wants people to think he is funny. And he wants people to think he is funny because he wants them to like him. But since we are getting to be better friends, he could just relax. He knows I like him already. Or maybe I was just so sugar-happy that I was out-whack-a-doodling Carson and he seemed super calm in comparison.

Now, I had really wanted Principal Carson's Mom to blow me away with deep and maybe even a little bit dangerous answers to my questions. I was thinking spies, wizards, secret clubs, paragraphs. I was hoping she even might say something like, "Okay, I will reveal to you the secret universal mystery of paragraphs, but once I do, your life will never be the same."

But get this! Her answers weren't life-changing at all! She just compared paragraphs to bread dough. She said that if you knead them right, they'll bake up good. But every loaf will be different because every baker is different, and every kitchen is different. Same with paragraphs. There is no magic formula.

But where's the universal mystery in that?

I think she could see that I was disappointed. She tried to make it up to me. (And this was really good, so I paid extra-close attention and wrote it in my notebook. I even had her repeat it.) She said, "What is important, Susie B., is that some people live their whole lives never thinking about paragraphs and how they work and what they do. To them, 'paragraph' is just another word, like 'foot' or 'banana.' The fact that you are thinking about this stuff is pretty impressive. Don't you think?"

Well . . . I mean . . . that did make sense. I guess I was being a little bit fabulous in noticing something that most people don't notice, and—for that—I do have to say thank you to my butterfly brain. It may not be so great at reading the directions for math problems that are way too complicated, but it does help you notice when people are talking nonsense, especially nonsense that most people accept without a second thought. And that is a good thing!

A little bit after that, Principal Carson's Mom got an emergency work phone call. It was going to take a while, so she told us to wander around. She'd find us when she was done.

We went back to the Picassos and sat down. Or

Carson sat. I kept sliding back and forth along the bench. We were across from this big black, white, and gray painting of a lady holding her elbow in one hand and leaning the knuckles of her other hand against her chin.

She looked beautiful, but not the kind of beautiful someone like Chloe would recognize. She wasn't thin. She was big, with wide shoulders and a curvy, strong body. She was amazing. Still, she looked sad. When I mentioned that to Carson, he nodded.

He got the same gleam in his eye that I get when I have to write, write, write, so I guess I shouldn't have been surprised when he pulled a sketchbook from his backpack. But I *was* surprised. I had always thought I was the only goofball who had to be totally prepared for my goofballness. But Carson had to be totally prepared for his goofballness too! I felt like, *Yeah for us!*

He offered me some paper.

I shook my head and watched him as he began to sketch the painting in front of us.

He nodded at the lady and told me that she was probably sad because Picasso was being a jerk to her.

Carson, of course, had said Picasso was a sexist doofus in his hero presentation, but now he told me more. Apparently, Picasso sucked everything he could out of the women in his life and then dumped them. Two of his partners even killed themselves.

My heart went twinge-boom-wow-boo. But what was I supposed to do with that information? Hate Picasso? Not hate Picasso? It was a nice painting. He was dead—just like all the other class heroes. Did it matter? My mind was getting all mixed up again, and, in this case, it didn't help that I was feeling so wiggly.

I muttered something like, "It's easier when you just know what people did, not who they were."

"Yeah," he answered. "People make no sense."

I got out my notebook and wrote that down.

Still drawing, he said very la-di-da casually, "Hey, how come you're eating lunch with Chloe and her friends now?"

I did not want to get into the yucky details of everything that was going on because—I don't know—those details maybe don't make me look too good. They make me look like a stinky sneak who will buddy up with mean people just to win elections, or a baby who will do anything to keep the best friend she's had since second grade, or a confused piñata who cannot even tell if she's getting whacked around.

So instead, I did this clever (but kind of rotten) thing that Lock does when Mom asks him how close he is to finishing his university-transfer applications. I put Carson on the spot. I knocked his question out of his brain by asking my own highly sensitive one.

Still sliding back and forth on the bench, I asked if he remembered when we ate lunch together.

He nodded, and I added, "I've been wondering. Who do you normally eat lunch with?"

This was actually a question that had been rattling around in my brain for a little while, but every time I thought of it, I would quickly shove it into the back of my mind. Because did I have a responsibility? That was the question behind the question. As Carson's friend—and especially as someone who Carson had helped more than once—did I have a responsibility to make sure that Carson was eating lunch with someone? And if he did not have someone to eat lunch with, did I have a responsibility to make sure that Carson ate with me and Joselyn—or me and Joselyn and Chloe, Rachelle, Rachel, and Rose—or more likely, just me? Those guys would never eat with Carson. See? That was the problem! Everything was already so weird with Joselyn. Adding Carson to the mix would definitely make it weirder.

But now, by pulling a Lock, I had asked the question, and it seemed like—whatever happened—one way or another, I was involved.

Carson didn't even stop drawing. He shrugged and said that he floated around or went to Soozee's clubs.

Now, everyone knows that some kids are floaters—and there is nothing wrong with being a floater. If you want to eat or hang out with one person one day, another person the next day, and another person the day after that, that is fine—as long as it's your choice, as long as you are floating because you love yourself some social variety. I've always thought that Soozee is that kind of floater.

The problem is when floating isn't a choice. The problem is when floating is another word for not having friends.

"Do you like floating?" I was really squirming now. I was just hoping that Carson would think it was because I was butterflyish and not out of cringey awkwardness.

He shrugged again, said it was okay.

I nodded. But you know what? I didn't know if I believed him. Listen, I see people frown when Carson makes his bird sounds. I see them roll their eyes when Mr. Springer asks him to stop drawing and focus on his work, or look at one another when he blurts something out in class, or when he gets so flappy that even his fidgets don't work and he starts climbing around on his chair or suddenly finds himself in the back of the room doing something he is not supposed to be doing. And I know how it feels to get those looks. The truth is, I get them too sometimes. If I had been at school right then? I would have been swimming in those looks.

I stared down at my notebook and started to doodle. What I should have said was, "Well, you know, you can always eat lunch with me." I was thinking about it. I was weighing the consequences of those words when Carson said, "It's better than eating with people who are mean."

Oh, dang! He went right there.

I put down my pencil, scooched over to him. "Chloe is mean, isn't she?"

He laughed a laugh of truth, and all that fog of doubt and confusion that had been hovering around the corners of my wiggly self lifted. My wiggliness even lifted. I was a laser beam of focus.

My eyes opened wider. "She's a real word bomber. Don't you think?"

"I don't know what that means," he said. "But it sounds right."

"Why don't other people see that she's mean?"

"Oh, they see it. They just don't care. It's better not to care."

Well, that didn't make sense to me at all. I asked him

what he meant. And I might not have this right word for word. But the gist of what he said was this: If you care, you have to do something, and what can you do?

I looked out at the painting in front of us, my mind going, *Boom! That's deep!*

"Wow. You are really smart," I said to Carson.

He shrugged again. "I'm glad you noticed."

I asked him one last thing. I used a tiny little mouse voice that probably sounded kind of insecure, but I needed to know. "Am I mean?"

"No," he spat, and he spoke with such surprise that I knew he meant it. "You're real. That's the best thing about you."

I looked some more at that painting and all its white, black, and gray. No Inner Light at all.

Picasso. What a jerk. He sucked all the Inner Light right out of that lady. But she had been somebody. She'd been a real person—as real as him. She deserved her Inner light. She had a right to her spark. Why had she given it away? Why had she let him take it? Why hadn't she done something?

I would have done something.

Double dang. Maybe I have to do something.

Dear NOT Susan B. Anthony:

I talked to Joselyn. I called her Sunday, after I'd had time to think about things. Here is what I told her:

She is my best spark.

She knows Chloe can be mean. Everyone knows Chloe can be mean. I'm not the one who is confused.

We couldn't let Chloe suck away our spark.

She had to choose: me or Chloe.

She chose Chloe.

Well, she didn't say that. She said, yes, Chloe sometimes blurts out things that aren't nice, but she doesn't mean half of them, and I'm a blurter too, so I should understand that better than anyone. She told me she'd had fun at Girl Scouts, and after Girl Scouts she had a sleepover with Chloe and the three Rs, and she didn't want to tell me because she didn't want to hurt my feelings, but there it was. She liked them. They liked her. They wanted her to join their Girl Scout troop and help at the bunny rescue.

It wasn't easy to hear. It all sounded pretty stabby-

stabby, even though her voice sounded more sorry-sorry. But I had planned out what I wanted to say, so I plowed ahead. "Well, I can't eat lunch with them."

"Well," she answered, "I like eating lunch with them."

So there you go. That was that.

Except it wasn't. Because after I was really quiet for a while, she also said this: "You know the Chloe vote was your only chance. You'll never win president now."

Dear REAL Susan B. Anthony:

I am worried about Monday.

I am worried about what will happen at lunch when I don't have Joselyn to spark me up.

I am worried that if Joselyn won't eat with me, and she doesn't take tap with me, will we still be friends? *Are* we still friends?

Was it easy to break away from your buddies over the Fifteenth Amendment? Was it like, *Skip-scoop, we were friends. Now we're not. No big deal. See you never?*

I mean . . . I guess your pal Elizabeth was still by your side, so you weren't alone or anything. But did it hurt? Did you feel it? Or was it like tearing off a Band-Aid, one big ouch and then pain-free? Or maybe even no ouch at all?

Shush! Don't answer. I'm still disgusted by you.

Dear REAL Susan B. Anthony:

When you were trying to convince everyone that women had the right to vote, did you ever feel like there were two of you? The first you was the regular one who everyone saw, the one who gave speeches and traveled on trains. The second you lived inside regular you. It was sparkless and cubist, like that sad, wonky woman in Picasso's painting, and it was like that because everyone was hating on the things regular you had to say. And that inner you was always poking regular you, trying to get your attention. And regular you was like, "Stay down, sad inner cubist me! I don't want to see you!"

"Of course I never felt that way," I hear you answering. "Failure is impossible! That's my motto. Hold on to your grit like it's gold!"

Well, aren't you perfect?

Not.

All day, I've been feeling like there are two of me. Cubist me and regular me. I finished my homework. I went to the store with Mom. I went for a bike ride with Dad. And all the while, sad cubist me kept pulling on my heart, saying, "Look at me!"

And regular me kept saying, "No! I will not look at you! If I look at you, you will make everyone else look at you. And no one wants to see you. You're too high-maintenance!"

Dear NOT Susan B. Anthony:

I was pretty darn mopey when I got to school this morning. I just knew it was going to be so awkward and weird when Joselyn and I saw each other, and I've always said that awkward and weird are just the worst. But guess what? They're not the worst! Being iced out is the worst! I know that now because that is what happened. Joselyn iced me out. When I got to school and said hi to her, she turned away and pretended I didn't exist.

Carson saw the whole thing, and when it was over, he said to me, "Whoa. That's cold."

But I couldn't answer because my lips were frozen together.

We went to class. I sat next to Carson. Mr. Springer started talking. What did he say? I have no idea. I just knew that there was no way that outer regular me was going to be able to keep sad inner cubist me hidden. Oh, I was trying. I was pushing her down real hard. But she was pushing back, and she was spiky and grabby in all her cubist ways. She was just looking for the right moment to break out and take over.

But then a miracle happened.

Mr. Springer said the only words in the world that could unplug my ears and tame inner cubist me, the only words that could shove gratitude and delight down her big, sad throat.

He said, "Student council candidates, I need you to go straight to the multipurpose room. Today you'll be practicing with *the big microphone*."

Oh, the words sounded so beautiful. It was like angels singing, but with jazz hands.

I stood up and my feet started walking. Without a look back, they walked out the door. They passed the other fifth-grade classes' doors. They passed Soozee and Matt Chan. And soon they were running down the hallway, sending my hair flying behind me.

I entered the multipurpose room.

There it was, on the stage: the big microphone of my dreams, the one all the student council presidents of years gone by have stood behind while belting out the Pledge of Allegiance. It was black, smooth, and connected to a shiny silver pole. It was glorious, more gorgeous than anything that jerk Picasso could have ever created.

Ms. Kim, the woman who directed the *Great American Presidents* play, was standing behind it, smiling as we all made our way inside.

Soozee came up to me. "Oh," she said in a shivery voice. "I don't really like speaking in public."

I looked at her, asked the obvious: "Why in the world would you run for student council if you didn't want to yak at a bunch of people who are being forced to listen to you?"

"To help," she said, as if that were an even more obvious answer than the one I'd given.

Ms. Kim had us sit down on the floor. She said she knew we had all been working hard on our speeches.

I thought, *You better believe it, sister!* Although, actually, I guess maybe I've more imagined how great it will be to stand on the stage and inspire people than I've figured out what to say. All I know for sure is that, when my speech ends, I'm gonna tap-dance right off the stage.

Joselyn asked if we would be running through our actual speeches.

Sad cubist me pinched my gut, noticing that Joselyn hadn't even sat near me. She was way over by her competition, Matt Chan.

But the lure of the big microphone kicked inner

cubist me's sadness down the road as Ms. Kim explained that she was just going to go over some pointers and then give everyone a few seconds to try the microphone for themselves.

Of course, she invited Dylan up to the stage to show us how it was done.

Beside me, Soozee let out a little moan.

My eyes bugged out as I turned to her in surprise. Soozee Gupta! Miss Friendly America! Who would have thunk it?

She saw me looking at her and blushed. "Sorry," she whispered. "I like Dylan. It's just that he gets chosen for so many things."

I nodded, shocked that—in her own way—Soozee was calling Dylan out for being a usual genius.

"But that's why I like my clubs," she said. "They're for everyone, not just the Dylans."

I had never really thought about it that way. The whole reason Joselyn had never been in the chess club was that it met after school, when she couldn't go. All the official clubs meet after school. But Soozee's clubs weren't official. She just made them up and did them when she wanted. And she did invite everyone.

Dylan was on the stage now.

Ms. Kim quieted us all again. Then she told us that

she and Dylan were going to demonstrate what *not* to do during our speeches. She whispered something to Dylan, and, louder—so we could hear—she told him to say his name and to tell us one thing he liked to do.

Bored as could be, he said, "My name is Dylan Rodriguez. I like to play soccer."

"Don't put your audience to sleep!" said Ms. Kim, faking a big yawn. "You've got to sound excited!"

Over and over again, she whispered things to Dylan, and he would show us all the things we shouldn't do onstage: We shouldn't speak too quickly into the microphone. We shouldn't speak too softly into the microphone. We shouldn't speak too loudly into the microphone. We shouldn't speak too close to the microphone. We shouldn't stand too far away from the microphone. We shouldn't be all hunched over. We shouldn't be all wiggly. We shouldn't play with our hands, or our hair, or our ears, or any jewelry.

Instead, when speaking into the big microphone, we should look calmly out at the audience. With our feet shoulder-width apart, and with our hands at our sides, we should remember all the shouldn'ts and say our speeches with confidence and enthusiasm.

Finally, she had Dylan introduce himself one last time, this time doing it right.

"Hi," he said, dazzling us with his cereal-commercial charm. "I'm Dylan Rodriguez! I like soccer!"

Soozee leaned next to me. She whispered, "I think we are going to lose."

I turned. She was smiling a very Soozee Gupta smile, but underneath the smile was something different. For a moment, it seemed like the sad inner cubist girl in me saw the sad inner cubist girl in her. And that was interesting, because one, I never knew Soozee had a sad inner cubist girl inside her, and two, I kind of liked her all the more for it.

Dylan came down, and one by one, Ms. Kim called us up to the stage so we could give it a try.

Everyone did okay.

Soozee seemed nervous, but not in a way that made me want to hide my face in my sweatshirt.

Of course, Matt strutted around like a star athlete.

Joselyn did so well that I felt happy, sad, and even a little jealous.

As for me . . . well, you are never going to believe this. The whole time I was waiting for my turn, I felt like a magnet that was being pulled to a refrigerator. Oh, I just wanted to go up to that big microphone so badly. And I didn't care what Ms. Kim said. I wasn't just going to let my hands hang by my sides. No way! I was going to hold that microphone like it was the best corn dog in the world. And I did! As soon as Ms. Kim called my name, I raced up to the stage. I pulled the microphone out of its stand before she could stop me.

Letting my voice ring throughout that giant multipurpose room, I very dramatically said, "I pledge allegiance to the flag of the United States of America."

"Perfect," said Ms. Kim, reaching out to take the microphone.

I scooted sideways. "And to the republic for which it stands."

Ms. Kim tried again to grab the microphone. "That's enough."

I ducked out of her reach and rushed to the other side of the stage. I knew I didn't have much time. "Save the polar bears!"

Ms. Kim yanked the microphone away.

I smiled out at all the other kids sitting on the floor. Some of them looked excited and surprised that I had been so good at holding tight to that microphone. Soozee even clapped and shouted, "Yes! Save the polar bears!" But most of them seemed bored or distracted—and I *know* distracted! Joselyn wasn't looking at me at all.

Ms. Kim leaned over me. Angrily, she explained that the mic needed to stay in the stand at all times and that if I removed it from the stand during my actual speech, I would be in big trouble.

I barely heard her. Because the weirdest thing in the history of weird things was happening to me.

I had always thought the big microphone would make me feel all glittery inside. And for the briefest second, when I was talking, it seemed like it would. But when I smiled out at the audience, I felt . . . nothing. I didn't feel glory. I didn't feel sparkly. I felt exactly the same as before I started. And it wasn't just the sad inner cubist me spoiling things. And it wasn't because Joselyn was ignoring me. It was about something bigger than both of those things. I just didn't exactly know what.

I zombie-walked off the stage.

When we were told we could go back to class, people came up and started talking to me.

Soozee told me that I had been a real natural up there.

Matt Chan, who I've never said a word to, said, "Boy, you really made Ms. Kim run!"

Even Dylan complimented me. He told me that I sounded very passionate, and that I needed to keep that passion going. "Be even bolder," he said. "Smile even wider."

Their words barely landed in my brain before flitting away. All I could think about was that nothing had changed. The big microphone hadn't sparked me up at all. It hadn't done anything, to anyone. I didn't understand. I still don't. Why didn't it feel the way I thought it would? Why didn't I feel . . . glory?

Dear REAL Susan B. Anthony:

Well, as usual, Lock knew the answer. I went and found him right when I got home from school. When I told him how the big microphone had let me down, he said I'd fallen for the oldest trick in the book: looking for love in a microphone.

He was like, "People will hear you when you talk into a microphone. They might even clap for you and tell you you're great. But that kind of love doesn't stick. It's like putting a Post-it note on your shirt. It's going to fall off." And that is a word-for-word quote, as I'm sure you guessed because there is no way I could make up baloney as good as that.

But Lock says it isn't baloney and that I need to stop comparing myself to others.

"That is your problem, right there," he said. "It's not that you're high-maintenance or low-maintenance. It's that you're always comparing yourself to others. You're always wanting what everyone else has. When you do that, you look for happiness outside yourself. You look for it in microphones or compliments or popularity. You can't help it. You need the world to tell you that you're as good as—or better than—anyone else. But even if the world tells you that, you won't really hear it—at least for long—because there will always be someone who seems to have more than you or is somehow better than you."

I wasn't having it. I shook my head. "No. I don't think anyone is better than anyone else. I just want things to be fair."

He spread out his hands. "Well, things aren't fair. And fairness isn't even really the problem. Justice is the problem. Is it fair when the fastest runner wins the race?"

I nodded.

"That's right. If I lose some race because the guy next to me is faster, that's fair. But did I lose because everyone got to wear superfast shoes but me? Well, that's unjust. When things are unjust, go ahead, be high-maintenance, complain, make a big deal. But you won't feel filled up because people are nodding at you. You'll feel filled up when you give your best to the world and then . . . let go."

"Let go?"

"Let go. If people clap, let that go. If people boo, let

that go. If someone is legit faster than you, well, wave goodbye and be on your way. Just give the world your best. Fill yourself up by being your best."

When I left Lock's room, I said I'd think about what he said, but I was just saying that to shut him up. I thought, *This time, Lock doesn't know what he is talking about. He is just making stuff up to make me feel better.*

But the more I thought about it, the more I realized that maybe Lock was right. I mean, I've tried fakey-faking. I've tried being low-maintenance. I've tried living every day with a sad inner cubist me. None of those things made me happy. You know what makes me happy? Supporting all the rights of all the people, polar bears, and paragraph writers. Maybe it's time that I went back to doing that and just tried not to worry so much about who was a usual genius, or being any kind of maintenance, or even whether people insult tap dancing. Maybe I should just try to give the world my best and let the rest go.

Here's what I've been wondering, though: Did you give the world your best, Susan B. Anthony?

I think you tried.

But did you ever think about the difference between fair and just?

See? That's where I think you messed it up. Like, if

you had been thinking more about the shoes and less about the winner, maybe you would have told that awful George Francis Train to go jump in a lake, and maybe you would have supported those Black suffragists and not thrown poor Frederick Douglass under the bus.

Fair and just. They're different things. That matters. And so I think I know what I need to do.

Dear NOT Susan B. Anthony:

I took down my campaign posters and put up new ones today. Oh, and they were glitterama! They were the most glitterama posters in the history of posters. I didn't break any rules. I only made two of them. I made sure they were twelve by eighteen inches and hung vertically. But they were the real me. The outside of each poster was an inch thick with golden glitter. On the inside of each poster there was writing in silver gel pen, and over the gel pen was a perfect dusting of rainbow glitter. Each poster said:

Susie B. for President

Susie B. is running for president but will probably lose because she is not popular and does not have the youth vote, but if she were president, she would know the difference between fair and just, and she would find a way to do these things:
Give all the people all the rights!
Help polar bears!

Let kids write paragraphs as long as they want!
Not let anyone suck away people's Inner Lights!
Vote for whoever you want! Student council is most
likely just a scam to get free kid labor. Boo! Boo! Boo!
Susie B. Out

It is true that that's a lot of words for a poster. Mom, Dad, and Lock all said so. They also said that putting those words, in that order, on a campaign poster was a very bad idea.

"No one will vote for you if you put that on your posters, especially with all that glitter," said Lock.

"People will think you are very angry if you put that on your posters," said Mom.

"Are you very angry?" said Dad.

You know what I said?

"Who cares?! I'm hanging these posters tomorrow morning."

Here's some credit for Mom. Even though she thought it was a bad idea, she got me to school half an hour early. And I took down my old posters and hung my new ones. Because I didn't care.

But someone did care. And that someone stole my posters!

I discovered it after I'd torn my old posters into pieces and thrown them away. I was on my way back to look at the new one I'd hung by the lunch tables when I ran into Carson. I dragged him over to see my new poster, and—boom—it was gone. We looked for it and couldn't find it, so we went to see my second poster. Boom! It was gone too!

I scanned the playground. Most of the kids were still streaming in through the gate. Others were lined up same as normal on their classroom lines. No one looked suspicious. No one looked like they were trying to hide anything. No one had a trail of glitter behind them.

Carson had a very shocked look on his face. I could tell he was as concerned as I was. He said, "Why would someone take down your posters?"

Exactly! That is exactly the question! First Chloe stole Joselyn. Now someone stole my posters. It was too much. I moped over to my line, feeling about as tall as dirt, my head swimming in disappointment. I just didn't understand it. It made no sense at all.

Those posters had been the one thing I'd been excited about, the one thing that made me feel like me. I thought people would see those posters and think, *Wow! Susie B. is telling it like it is! She's being super real! You know what? I'm probably not going to vote for her, but she is at least giving the world her best.*

At least . . . I hoped certain ex–best friends who are no longer talking to me might think that.

But now no one will think that because they will never see how glitter-glorious they were.

Carson wouldn't stop bugging me about making new posters, but I told him no way. I'd used up all my glitter making the new ones. If I couldn't have a poster with glitter, I didn't want one at all. What did it matter? I was going to lose anyway. There was nothing fair about it. There was nothing just about it. Everything about it smelled of evil.

And I'll tell you this. As soon as I realized that, I was mopey no more. I was mad. I was angry. I WAS AN ANGRY GIRL. And I was not going to hide my angry girl for anything.

I said to Carson, "I will find who stole my posters. I will find them, and I will shake my fist at them, and I will show them what high-maintenance means, and they will be sorry!"

And you know what, Susan B. Anthony? THEY WILL!!!!

Dear NOT Susan B. Anthony:

Strange mischief to report! Chloe is back to being all friendly to Dylan. When we were walking into class this morning, she was like, "Oh, Dylan, I like your shoes. They are very . . . festive."

He grunted at her like always and started to walk faster.

She followed him and was like, "You'll be such a good president. You'll be very *presidential*."

Aha! Don't think I missed that one. Get it? Presidential? That's the line from my old posters. She was hinting. *She* did it! She tore down my posters! Maybe Joselyn told Chloe I didn't want to eat with them and she felt insulted. Or—is it possible?—maybe Chloe saw my poster and thought, *Hey! This poster is actually so real that maybe everyone will vote for Susie B. It will be just like when Dylan wowed us all by telling us what a jerk Steve Jobs was. People will be so surprised that they'll clap and clap.* But she didn't want them to clap and clap. She wanted Dylan to win. Because she was always going to vote for him anyway. She just wanted to scare him a little by making him think she might vote for me. So he'd appreciate her more. That's the whole reason she was being nice to Joselyn and me. But when she realized my new posters might actually get people to vote for me, she said to herself, "I'm queen. Dylan is king. I need to protect him!"

Oh my gosh. I bet that is what happened! Errrgh! When I find proof that she ruined my posters, she is going down.

Dear NOT Susan B. Anthony:

It's all making more sense now.

I've been thinking about something Joselyn once said to me. It was one of the times I was losing to her at chess. The game had been going on for a while, and I was starting to feel antsy and hyper and like I couldn't sit there one more minute. So I started to do some tap-dance moves between turns.

Joselyn didn't like that. Frustrated, she snapped, "You should like chess, Susie B. The most powerful piece is the queen. She gets to boss around the whole board. It's very girl-power."

I don't remember what I said or what we did after that. But I do remember thinking, *Way to go, queen!*

But you know what? I think Joselyn was wrong. The most powerful piece is the king. Sure, he can only move one square at a time, and—sure—every opponent's piece is coming for him, but every one of his own pieces is protecting him. Their entire reason for existence is to protect him. And no one can get mad at him. They can't be all, "Urgh! You took my bishop," or "Urgh! You took my knight." But you can say that to the queen. You can say that to every other piece on the board. And all the while you are blaming the other pieces, you are not noticing how the king gets to kill off all his kingdom just to stay in his one little square without doing a darn thing.

Stupid Dylan.

And I had been thinking of being nice to him and everything. It had been part of my whole give-my-best-and-let-it-go plan. Usual genius? Got your face on a cereal box? Most popular person in the world? Who cared? Not me! I am happy just being me! I'm letting that go. I'm better than all that.

Oh, but that is over now. Chloe destroyed my posters *for him*. All he had to do was sit there and do nothing while everyone around him made sure he didn't lose his crown.

Oh, they are both gonna get it!

Dear REAL Susan B. Anthony:

Here is an unexpected twist. Carson made me new posters. They were hanging up when I got to school today. He was standing next to the one near the lunch tables when I walked through the gate.

He screamed, "Check it out!" and when I got closer, he added, "Ta-da!"

I could hardly believe it. It was beautiful! It looked kind of like my original poster but much more artistic. Instead of a photo of my face, he'd made a pastel drawing of me flexing my arm muscles, and instead of having glitter near the edges, he'd put a ton of glitter on the word "Presidential." And that was the best part, because it meant he remembered how sad I'd been that all my good glitter skills had gone to waste.

It's probably the nicest thing anyone has ever done for me.

He took me over to see the other poster he'd made. This one hung near our classroom. It looked almost identical to the first, except—instead of me flexing my arm muscles—I had my hands on my hips and wore a Superman cape.

Soozee came up to us, oohing and aahing. She said she'd been wondering what had happened to my posters, then added, "You are so smart to mix things up. People love variety. I wish I'd thought of that."

Dylan came up to us. He was like, "This is really good. I bet you'll get a lot of votes with this." He looked some more at the poster, and then—surprising me even more—he said, "You're a great artist."

I explained that Carson made the poster.

And Dylan was all, "Carson! You're a genius!"

I was like, *Whoa, dude! Stop! It's hard to be mad at you for being king of the chessboard when you are being so nice.* But all I said was, "Yeah, Carson is amazing."

And then who do you think came up to us?

Ha! Chloe! And she was with Joselyn.

Chloe was like, "Oh . . . a new poster. It's . . . cute?"

"It's brilliant," I said, showing her my eyes of death. "No one better take it down, either. If they do, they will be very sorry. And that is not high-maintenance talk. That's grit."

Chloe gave Joselyn a very confused look and asked why someone would take down my posters.

I was thinking, *Oh! She is an expert fakey fake! That is for sure.*

Joselyn shrugged, and the two of them headed for our class line.

I looked back at Dylan. His face had turned red. He seemed nervous, and I felt a little worse that I'd been holding his being king of the chessboard against him. Obviously, he hated Chloe bugging him all the time. I thought, *Maybe I'm being unfair.*

He said, "So . . . anyway, with these good posters, maybe you might win because, you know, you are also a pretty good public speaker. But can I say one thing to you? Okay, I'm going to say one thing. Just—when you give your speech—remember the rules, the school rules about the election. That's really important."

I said, "Okay."

But he hadn't quite stopped talking, and he kept talking.

"The thing about the rules is . . . you know . . . if you make promises you can't keep—like if you say you are going to do something as president that the president can't do—they'll kick you out of the election. Then . . . how can you win if you're kicked out? Right?"

I nodded, and I was thinking that he should be wrapping things up. Mr. Springer was walking to the line, and we weren't even over there yet.

But Dylan didn't wrap it up. He was looking only at me as he said, "For sure, don't mention polar bears or paragraphs in your speech—especially not paragraphs, because that's teaching stuff, and the president can't change teaching stuff. Remember?"

"Okay," I said, starting to feel that something wasn't right with Dylan, that he was about to freak out or something.

I looked down. My eyes drifted to Dylan's shoes. They were running shoes, and they must have been pretty new because they were bright white. Near the side of one of them was a smudge of golden glitter. It wasn't much, a curved line more than a blob. But it was there. I was looking at it. And I realized that Chloe had been right. That glitter did make his shoes look a little festive. I was thinking, *That's not very Dylan Rodriguez to add a festive smudge of glitter to his shoes.* And then I was thinking . . . *How did he know I was going to talk about polar bears and paragraphs in my speech? My posters were taken down before school even started. . . .*

And then it hit me. It was him! He was the evil genius who'd stolen my glitterama posters! That's how he knew about my speech! I'd practically written it right on them.

My mouth dropped open. I looked up at him in shock!

He stopped midsentence. His eyes got wider. He knew I knew. And there it was: guilt! Oh, it was written on his face like a bunch of letters to a dead lady.

Suddenly, Dylan broke from where he stood and rushed to the line.

It was only then that I noticed he had his Steve Jobs posters with him. He had a new angel one. (Ha! He'd shown us all along what a poster-ruiner he was! He'd shown us the day he'd torn his first angel Steve Jobs poster in half.) He also had his old devil Steve Jobs poster. Why? I didn't know. It didn't matter. What mattered was that this was an injustice that could not go unanswered. It was one thing for Dylan Perfect Rodriguez to have all the luck in the world. It was another thing for him to squash my voice.

Every muscle in my body tightened.

Suddenly, Soozee was touching my elbow.

"You okay?"

I pulled away, shouting, "I will have justice!" I tried to catch up to Dylan. Of course, he is also perfect at being fast, and he was whipping through people back and forth until he was right behind Mr. Springer.

I skipped the line completely, trying to head Dylan off at the classroom, but time and my slow feet were against me. When Mr. Springer opened the door, Dylan was the first one inside. By the time I got in, he was in his chair on the far side of the room. I moved toward him as Mr. Springer—always having Dylan's back—pointed toward my chair and told me to take a seat.

I sat.

Dylan wasn't looking at me, so he didn't know that my eyeballs were burning a hole into his head. But at the same time, he knew.

Carson slid into his seat. "What's going on?"

Before I could explain, Mr. Springer snapped his fingers and called my name. Was I paying attention? Could I pay attention?

A butterfly can always pay attention to a snake.

Mr. Springer started to get us ready for the Hero Parade, which I had sort of forgotten was this morning. But that was okay. My float was ready. It had a little paper doll of you on top, Susan B. Anthony. I had made it myself. It was holding a picket sign that said, "Votes for Women! (But also I'm a little bit racist!)"

Then Mr. Springer explained that—for the first time ever—he had decided we should finish the Hero Parade with an inspiring student speech. And who would give that speech? Dylan! Because Dylan's speech had been so amazing and good and we had all loved it so much, and didn't we all want to hear it again? And didn't we want our fourth-grade audience to hear it? Wouldn't that be a great opportunity for them? Couldn't we give Dylan a hand? Wouldn't we all do that right now? To show Dylan our support?

Dylan looked up as everyone started to clap. If he was red before, he was purple now. His eyes bulged and he tried to smile.

"Oh, don't be nervous," Mr. Springer told him. "The fourth graders will love you!"

Dylan looked over at me and saw my glare of doom. He gulped and looked back down.

Still staring at Dylan, I pulled my notebook from my pocket. I tore out one of the little pieces of paper.

"What are you doing?" Carson sounded nervous. He didn't know what was going on, but he knew I was mad.

I whispered, "I'm blowing it all up."

With a stub of a pencil I wrote, "Dylan thinks he is the usual genius of class, but really he is just a sneaky snake of an attention hog. Oink, oink. Pass it on."

I turned around and gave the note to Rachelle, who took one peek at my expression and passed it on without even reading it. The note moved on and on and on. And the mood of the class changed. Kids started looking at Dylan out of the corners of their eyes, and some of them looked like they didn't know what to think, and some of them looked like they felt bad for Dylan, and some of them looked spiteful and happy at the same time.

Then, all of a sudden, it was time for the parade. We took our floats and went outside to line up on the blacktop.

The fourth-grade classes were already waiting for us, and—even though this was not advertised as a family event—a few parents had shown up too, including Dylan's entire cheering squad. We'd all seen them so many times that we recognized them by sight. His parents were there. His grandparents and step-grandparents were there. Even his aunt, his aunt's twin babies, and his two older brothers—who must have been pulled out of their own schools just for this—were there.

I glared at them all.

But then I noticed that something was going on. Chloe was in the back of the line. She was standing next to Dylan. She was showing him the note. I saw her look up at me, a sick little smile on her face.

I looked hard at her and did a classic tap-dance dig, toe, step, heel.

The sick smile on her face got bigger.

The parade started. We pulled our floats and followed Mr. Springer in a loop around the blacktop.

When we were done, Mr. Springer called up Dylan.

There he was, walking over and taking his posters from Mr. Springer, looking like every bad thing that could happen to a person had just happened to him. *Good*, I thought. *Let him suffer.*

I began to tap-dance in place. The whole time, I stared at Dylan and sent him the silent message: *you are going down.*

He started to give his speech, saying again all the amazing things Steve Jobs had done. But you could tell he wasn't into it. You could tell his mind was somewhere else, somewhere I had sent it.

I glanced at his family. They were frowning, even the twin babies. They knew something was wrong.

I glanced at Mr. Springer. He was frowning. He knew something was wrong.

Suddenly, there was Chloe, standing at his side, handing him the note. They both looked up and scanned the circle where we stood.

Chloe pointed at me, not even bothering to hide how happy she was to tattle.

Mr. Springer caught my eye.

I stopped tap-dancing, shrugged, and he sighed.

Dear REAL Susan B. Anthony:

At lunchtime, Mr. Springer arranged the circle of chairs like this: one for him, one for Dylan, one for me. Right away, the questions started. Had I written the note? Why had I written the note? Why would I do such a thing? What had Dylan ever done to deserve such treatment? Had I thought about his feelings? Would I like it if someone wrote a note like that about me? Was I sorry? Didn't I think I should be sorry?

I glanced at Dylan. He wasn't purple anymore. Or nervous. If anything, he looked . . . hopeful.

Look at him, I thought. *He can't wait to see me get in trouble. What a Picasso!*

Well, I was not about to be Dylan's pawn. He wasn't my king. There was no way I was taking the blame for this. I banged my fist on my thigh. "No," I told Mr. Springer. "I am not sorry! Because Dylan started it."

Mr. Springer gave me the same look he gave me after my hero speech. He said, "You seem very angry. I can't hear you when you're so angry."

The words spilled right out. "You never hear me, Mr. Springer."

He blinked, took a second, then said, "Well . . . okay . . . I'm listening now."

So I vomited up the whole ugly mess. I said how Dylan had stolen the new posters I'd made and how I'd figured it out. Then, because I couldn't stop myself, I talked about the donuts, and the Oreos, and the hidden moves, and how the king is the most powerful chess piece because the queen does all his dirty work—and I think I lost Mr. Springer there—and the difference between what is fair and what is just.

All the time I was talking, I could see that Mr. Springer didn't believe me. He didn't believe me one bit. He'd already decided that I was the butterfly brain who got mad all the time, and Dylan was the usual genius who could do no wrong.

Finally, when I stopped talking, he said, "Dylan, did you do the things Susie B. said? Did you try to bribe voters? Did you destroy her posters?"

I knew Mr. Springer was just waiting for Dylan to shake his head and say, "I don't know what Susie B. is talking about, Mr. S."

But Dylan didn't do that. Dylan looked down at the floor. Then, he nodded.

Mr. Springer tried to cover his surprise, but I saw it!

"There you go," I muttered. "Another hero bites the dust."

Mr. Springer glanced at me, confused. But then my words seemed to sink in. He bit down on his lip. For a second, it looked like he might laugh. Instead, he cleared his throat.

"Dylan," he said softly. "Why would you do those things?"

Dylan shook his head, shrugged.

The room grew quiet again.

But then, the truth came out. Dylan told us everything, and you are never going to believe what he said—I'll never forget it.

For a second his face got all purple again, and in a surprisingly Susie B.–like fashion, he yelled, "I don't want to be student council president!"

He admitted it right there in that circle, right in front of Mr. Springer and me. He said he *never* wanted to be student council president, just like he'd never wanted to sing a solo in first grade, or play George Washington, or perform Martha Washington's song, or even be on boxes of Bitty Donut Nature Crunch cereal. He hates all that stuff. All he really wants to do is play soccer and become an engineer one day.

But he did all those things because his million-percent-supportive family made him. Apparently, they have your same motto: "Failure is impossible!"

That's what I wanted to tell you, Susan B. Anthony. They stole your motto! But they also changed the meaning. For you, "failure is impossible" was about justice (even though you weren't always just). For them, it is about winning. They want to win at everything they try. It is very important to them. And if they don't win . . . I don't know. I guess it's bad.

The point is, Dylan just couldn't take it anymore. He thought he'd get kicked right out for giving people donuts. When he didn't, he came up with a different plan: lose. He thought maybe I'd beat him when I was buddying up to Chloe. But then he saw my new posters with all the writing about rights and polar bears and stuff. He thought I'd be booted from the election for making campaign promises I couldn't keep. So he tore my posters down and suggested to Carson that he make me new ones. Not that Carson even realized it. Dylan was so sneaky about it that Carson thought he'd come up with the idea by himself. And that was why Dylan was giving me advice about my speech. He didn't want me to do anything that might increase his chances of winning.

But he didn't stop there.

Get this! I was just his second-best hope! He was really counting on Soozee beating him since she has the youth vote (he'd figured it out too) and knows lots of people from her clubs. He'd even been telling his closest friends to vote for her!

When Dylan finally finished, Mr. Springer was rubbing his forehead like he had to help all this shocking information get into his brain. And then finally, he let out a big ol' sigh.

You can probably guess what came next.

Dylan is out of the election. Matt Chan is out of the election. And I am out of the election. We made bad decisions. We got the boot.

And you know what I think?

Thank goodness it's over.

Dear REAL Susan B. Anthony:

Wouldn't you know it? It wasn't over.

There was a little matter of parents being phoned.

And Matt Chan calling me a tattletale.

And Chloe snarking that I was a weirdo.

And me telling Chloe to go bob for pineapples.

And Joselyn telling us both to grow up.

By afternoon recess, the whole school knew what had happened. It was quite the scandal, believe you me. People were all whisper-whisper-choosing-sides. In most cases, the sides people chose had nothing to do with the truth of what happened and everything to do with who they were already friends with.

But what did that matter to me? My best friend had already ditched me. And what did I care about the kids who had wanted to vote for Matt or Dylan? They could scowl at me until the cows came home for all I cared. That was their game, not mine.

Still, I was a'stewing. I was a'stewing good. I was sitting on a bench, thinking about life and unfairness and injustice and everything bad. Soozee came by, told me she was sorry things hadn't worked out. Carson came by, asked if I wanted to watch him eat an ant. In the distance Joselyn played basketball with her new pals.

And then who do you think came and sat by me?

Dylan.

He said he just needed to know one thing about the note. "What's a 'usual genius'?"

I explained, adding, "It's nothing personal. But you are as usual genius as they come."

We were quiet for a minute. Then he asked if I wanted to walk around.

So we walked. We walked around the whole schoolyard, and when we were done, we did it again.

You know what?

It was totally fine.

I never thought I'd have much to say to a usual genius, but it turns out we have some things in common. His family has him so busy trying to be the best at stuff that he is screen-deprived too. Plus, he loves to write, and he used to keep a notebook just like me, but now he records all the good lines he hears on his phone, which is another reason I deserve a phone, if you ask me.

"I liked your hero speech," he told me. Looking a

little guilty, he said that he knew I hadn't copied his. "You couldn't have copied! You'd written that Susan B. Anthony was a two-faced biddy right on your poster."

"I know!" I said, feeling all over again how much that whole incident had hurt. "But that is the problem with usual geniuses. They always get the credit. They always get everything." I peeked at him from the corner of my eye. I wasn't trying to be mean, but it was the truth, and I believed he needed to hear it.

He nodded. But then he kind of put me in my place by saying, "I get that. But, you know, I do work hard, really hard."

It was my turn to look a little guilty. I'd never thought about how hard Dylan worked. Then again, how was I to know? He doesn't sit near me, and—until now—we'd barely talked.

"You work hard. You're smart. And, let's face it, you really hit that high note in that Martha Washington solo. Plus, now it turns out you're actually nice." I threw my hands in the air. "I guess you *are* perfect."

His face turned red and he shook his head, insisting—like a totally perfect person—that he wasn't perfect.

Funny enough, that got us back to talking about the Hero Project. I explained that the one thing that still really annoyed me was how all the heroes could be so perfect and so not-perfect at the exact same time. It was almost like they were wanting us to smack them in the face.

That had been bugging him, too, but his very smart aunt—the one with the twins—had explained it.

He asked if I knew what a paradox was.

Well, what do you think?

Of course not!

"Don't feel bad," he said. "I'd never heard it either until my aunt said it."

In case it's new to you, too, Susan B. Anthony, I will tell you: a paradox is when something is both one thing and an opposite thing at the same time.

Now, I know what you're thinking. You are thinking, "Paradoxes sound really stupid. How could something be one thing and an opposite thing at the same time?"

I know! I was thinking the same thing. And I told Dylan that.

But Dylan threw the example of you right in my face! "On the one hand," he said, "Susan B. Anthony was a hero who did heroic, important justice stuff. But on the other hand, she did some really unjust stuff too. She is a hero and not a hero at the same time. A paradox."

Dylan's aunt says most people are paradoxes.

I told him his aunt sounds a lot like Lock. When I

explained why, he said everyone in his family is a Lock.

Oh my goodness, I thought. *I love Lock, but a whole family of them? That sounds tiring.*

The bell rang, and we headed back to class, both of us grateful—I think—that if people were going to whisper-whisper at us, now they'd have to do so at both of us together.

I have to say, though, that I really liked the word "paradox." All day long I kept thinking about it and rolling it around in my mouth. All of a sudden, a light switch turned on in my head! I started to think about all the people I knew and the ways that they were paradoxes too. Like, Mom is a paradox because she is always bad-mouthing sugar, but she also has a secret stash of her own candy. And Lock is a paradox because he is loaded with grit, but sometimes his grit abandons him. Even Chloe is a paradox because she is a big word bomber, but she also feeds the homeless and volunteers with rescue bunnies.

Was I a paradox? It didn't seem possible. I'd tried to be old me. I'd tried to be lots of new mes. Did that make me a paradox? I couldn't see it. But maybe you can't see your own paradoxness. Maybe it's like how you can't see the back of your own head.

Or maybe I just wasn't a paradox.

But then I thought, *Wait . . . if most people are para-doxes, and I'm not a paradox, isn't that a paradox too?*

Kaboom, baby!

That was my mind getting blown away!

The point is, Susan B. Anthony, I will never forgive you for not supporting the Fifteenth Amendment and Black suffragists, but I do admit that you were a fighter and you did good stuff too. You played the game the only way you knew how, and you made some pretty terrible moves in the process. You are a paradox, just like most people, maybe even me.

Dear REAL Susan B. Anthony:

Hello. It's been a while. That's because I missed a few days of school so that my parents and I could visit the universities that have said, "Yes, Lock! We love you! Please come study here!"

That's right! It turns out that Lock pulled a little trick. He finished his transfer applications in secret so that Mom wouldn't be all, "Let me see! Did you finish? How is it going?"

And now he is doubling down on all his classes because he is for sure moving on in January. I don't know where he'll be—and I'll miss him a ton—but the university he chooses better be prepared. He'll Lock them down good if they try any funny business.

You're probably saying, "Enough about that, Susie B.! I've been worried ever since you called me a paradox. Are you sure you were cool with the whole student council disaster? Are you like, what, Dylan's girlfriend now? And how are things with Joselyn and even Old Fakey Fake?

Uggh.

Fine.

First of all, yes. I'm cool about the election stuff. I wasn't cool with my parents taking my little bit of screen time away from me for two weeks over the note, but . . . I get it.

Second of all, gross! Of course, I'm not Dylan's girlfriend! For someone who cared about women's rights, you have some really old-fashioned ideas. (But you know what? So does Chloe! And I think she's been a little bit nervous that Dylan "likes" me ever since she saw us walking on the blacktop. I love it! Let her stress about it. That's my best revenge.)

Third of all, as for Joselyn . . . well, stop being so gossipy. It's none of your business!

All you really need to know is that I am back at school, and even though I thought the Hero Project ended with the Hero Parade, I guess I was wrong. Today we are supposed to write to you using three of our spelling words, and we are supposed to write those words in all caps so that Mr. Springer can find them easily on the page. And we do not need to write in paragraph form at all. We can just go crazy because Mr. Springer wants us to be creative, and he knows that some of us actually do understand the not-so-universal mystery of paragraphs and can be trusted to write GORGEOUS paragraphs of whatever length we want.

But that is not my sentence about GORGEOUS. My sentence about GORGEOUS is that GORGEOUS is an evil word that should be banned from spelling tests. How can anyone possibly be expected to remember how to spell that silly word when the first *g* makes a regular *g* sound, and the second *g* makes a *j* sound and is then followed by three entirely different vowels?

I will also say that the word BEAUTIFUL is not much better. Who would invent a word with EAUTI in the middle? What kind of messed-up business is that? But even though it is also a silly word, BEAUTIFUL is great for describing polar bears. And I used it to describe them in our new Justice Club. That's right! I started a club. Actually, Soozee and I did it together. It was my idea, but I asked her to help since she is a club-starting expert, and she said yes because she has not let the power of being president go to her head.

"A club?" you're saying. "That's not like you!"

Well, now it is, Susan B. Anthony. I'm a work in progress, just like everybody else.

Soozee did warn me that the club won't last. She says they never do. People get bored, wanna try something new.

But that's okay. Because guess what? Between me, Carson, and Soozee, we've got a million ideas for other clubs. Like a Diversity Club, and a Words Matter Club, and an Arts Club. We will try club after club after club until we find one that sticks and does good work. Because—duh—you don't have to be president to make the world a better place. But you do have to do stuff, and you can't just talk about it.

And if that makes people think we are high-maintenance, we will say, "People aren't cars. They don't need maintenance, but they do need you to not be a jerk."

"Ummmm," I hear you saying. "Is Joselyn in the club?"

Oh my gosh! You are so nosy!

I'm super glad you and Elizabeth Cady Stanton were sparking each other until the bitter end. Yes, I thought it would be like that with me and Joselyn too, but . . . it seems I was wrong.

Am I sad that Joselyn is still hanging out with Chloe and the three Rs?

Obviously.

Is there still a sad inner cubist girl in me who gets all pokey every time I see them eating lunch or playing basketball?

I guess. But it's getting better. I've got Carson, and even Soozee, and a little bit Dylan. And I've got my grit. Maybe, for a while, that will have to be my spark.

I will say this, though. Today in class, I noticed that Joselyn wasn't wearing her ADORABLE worry-doll earrings.

I thought to myself, *Joselyn loves those earrings. Her grandma gave them to her. I think the only thing that would get her to take them off would be word bombing.*

So, at lunch, I went straight up to her at Chloe's table. I very casually smiled and said, "Hey, I just wanted to say that I miss seeing your ADORABLE worry-doll earrings. I have always liked them."

Rachelle said, "Yeah, where are your earrings? I like them too."

Chloe's cheeks turned a little pink, and she started to fiddle with a Ziploc baggie full of carrots.

And I thought, *Wah-ha! That's how you deal with a word bomber!*

I went and joined Carson and Soozee. We had a lot to talk about. We're planning a bake sale for polar bears, and we have to decide what to sell. For sure, there will be many sugary snacks, which no one can prevent because the sale is going to be in front of Soozee's house and so the school—and my mom—can't do anything. Psych on you, sugar haters!

Still, I couldn't help but look back at Joselyn, and you know what? When she saw me, she smiled a little. Then she turned back to Chloe and the three Rs and started talking.

So, who knows what will happen there?

Dear REAL Susan B. Anthony:

Well, this is it. This really is my last letter to you because the Hero Project is officially over, and while it has been nice (and not so nice), I have to admit that I'm glad I'm done. I'll still keep writing, of course. This butterfly brain isn't going to let me stop! But I think this is my last letter to you.

This is our final journal prompt: make a top-ten list of the best things you learned during this project.

Hooray! No one loves a top-ten list more than me. Here goes:

1. Susan B. Anthony: you believed in equality, but—surprisingly—you did not believe in it enough.

2. People, like math problems involving trains, are complicated. And that is because people are paradoxes.

3. Paragraphs may not be mysterious, but they aren't cookie cutters, either.

4. Even usual geniuses have problems.

5. Fair and just are not the same.

6. It's better to eat alone than to eat with people who treat you rotten.

7. But it's even better to have friends who stand up for you.

8. Sometimes you have a sad inner cubist kid inside you. That's okay.

9. If you don't like the game, make a new one.

10. Don't be a jerk.

11. Your Inner Light is yours. Hold it tight.

Acknowledgments

Dear Reader:

Thank you so much for reading this book!

I don't know if you know this, but it takes a lot of people to make a book, and I am so lucky that I get to thank them here.

First things first: thank you to my editor, Alex Borbolla. We should all be so lucky to have a collaborator and cheerleader like Alex. She makes my work better in ways that delight and inspire me.

Rebecca Vitkus also made this book better. You know how? She found all the typos and mistakes (including really embarrassing ones about how to spell Helena Rubinstein and where Susan B. Anthony was born). Clare McGlade and Alison Velea helped a lot with this, too. I'm so glad we had their help!

Do you like the cover illustration? I love it! It was done by Beverly Johnson. And how about the awesome design of the whole book? That's thanks to the wonderful Karyn Lee. Other people at Atheneum Books for Young Readers (the publisher of this book) also helped bring this book to you. I am grateful to all of them.

Thank you also to my agent, Tracy Marchini. She is the person who sold my book to Atheneum. I couldn't do what I do without her. Huzzah for Tracy!

Now, you are probably wondering how I know so much about Susan B. Anthony. What do you think? I read a bunch of books! Here are a few that really helped me: Lynn Sherr's *Failure Is Impossible: Susan B. Anthony in Her Own Words* (Times Books), Judith E. Harper's *Susan B. Anthony: A Biographical Companion* (ABC-Clio), and *The Oxford Companion to United States History*, edited by Paul S. Boyer (Oxford). Additional information, including facts about the perfect/not perfect heroes mentioned in this book, came from assorted websites, my favorites of which were www.susanb.org (the website of the Susan B. Anthony Museum and House) and www.Monticello.org (which will tell you everything you ever wanted to know about Thomas Jefferson). Thank you, historians! Thank you, historical societies and organizations!

Meg Miller, Nancy Matthews, Michelle and Ron, Katherine Bleakley, and Ronna Mandel have gone above and beyond the call of duty to support my writing. I am lucky to know them! I am likewise lucky to have Steve Finnegan, Elizabeth Finnegan, and Mary Finnegan in my life. They do so much for me. An extra word about Mary: she has become my first and one of my most valued readers. This book is dedicated to her because she is awesome.

Susie B. learns that you can't change much of anything without the help of others. Remember that, reader. Don't let your people slip away.